DEEP FREEZE

A StormWatch Novel

VICKI HINZE

Magnolia Leaf Press

Cover Design by VK Hinze

MAGNOLIA LEAF PRESS

Print Edition 2019. ISBN: 978-1-939016-35-5
Electronic Edition 2019. ISBN: 978-1-939016-38-6

MAGNOLIA LEAF PRESS
First Edition June 2019
Printed in the USA

DEDICATION

*To those who routinely put their
lives on the line for the rest of us.
Some debts can never be repaid,
but never doubt they are noted
with enormous gratitude.
Blessings!
Vicki*

ACKNOWLEDGMENTS

As always in creating a new series, there are many to thank for sharing their gifts and talents. Heartfelt gratitude to series plotting partner and series co-creator, Debra Webb, and to the esteemed authors who breathed life into the vision, Rita Herron, Regan Black, Peggy Webb, and Cindy Gerard. Incredible women and masterful authors all. We've shared an awesome adventure and what a blessing it has been to share it with all of you!

I would also like to thank the incredibly insightful author, Kathy Carmichael, for our hours of discussions on high-containment labs and emotional deep wells in dark places. Your steadfast support is without measure.

CONTENTS

PORTAL 3 NEWS

Tuesday, December 17th

Darcy Keller stood on the side of the road in the blowing snow and checked her earpiece, watching for her cameraman's cue. He counted down the last three seconds on his fingers. The anchor at the station segued to Darcy for the live shot.

"A severe weather alert has been issued for our viewing area. Holly is the worst storm in eighty years, and she's earning the title," Darcy began. "Fatalities and extensive damage are being reported in Montana.

"This morning, an abrupt jog has turned the storm to Colorado. Specifically, onto you, Portal. The weather is deteriorating rapidly. As you can see behind me, whiteout conditions are already occurring. High winds and a mix of snow and ice are making travel extremely dangerous and next to impossible. Authorities are advising you get where you're going now and settle in.

"For the last several hours, flights have been halted in

Denver and diverted to Portal International Airport. We're about five miles from PIA now, and it's taken hours to get this far. All along our path, we've witnessed cars spinning and sliding off the road. An eighteen-wheeler jack-knifed near the intersection of Interstates 25 and 76. The driver is critically injured. Stranded motorists have abandoned their vehicles and are seeking shelter on foot despite being warned to stay with their vehicles. Temperatures are plummeting. We expect subzero within the hour. Roads are closed to all but emergency vehicles and will remain shut down until after the storm passes. The National Guard has been activated to assist stranded drivers but, be warned, if the winds get much higher, they, too, will be sidelined, as will emergency responders.

"Over 1800 flights have been canceled at DIA in Denver. Now, I've just been advised, the diversionary airport in Portal has closed. With over 5,000 stranded travelers, Portal International is well over capacity. Our crew has been trying to make the typically thirty-minute trek from the station to PIA for over two and a half hours.

"At the moment, authorities are uncertain how many are without power, though they expect the number will be extraordinarily high by tomorrow morning due to ice and near hurricane-strength winds.

"We'll be on-site at PIA—Portal International—with live updates as soon as possible. Authorities urge residents to exercise extreme caution. In all of Portal's recorded history, we have not seen a storm like this. It's critical to your safety and your family's that you listen to the authorities. Follow their advice. Hunker down, Portal. And stay tuned for the latest weather alerts.

"A personal observation: Conditions are already rough out here. They are going to get a lot worse before they get better. Avoid taking risks, check your emergency supplies, and stay safe. Remember, things can be replaced. You can't.

"This is Darcy Keller for Portal 3 News. Back to you in the studio..."

CHAPTER ONE

1440 (2:40 PM)

WHY DO weathermen and women stand outside in near hurricane-strength winds, blowing snow and ice, to relay Emergency Weather Alerts, reporting dangerous weather conditions, and urge residents to stay indoors?

Emma Miller stood in a cluster of stranded travelers staring up at the TV screen in the Portal Airport terminal unable to think of one good reason for a person to put themselves through that misery. From Darcy Keller's involuntary twitches, the ice pelting her stung through her heavy red coat and the hood covering her head. Worse, she was clearly pregnant. A couple standing near Emma questioned the wisdom of Darcy Keller being out in the storm, risking a fall or injury. Silently, Emma agreed. The ice was slick. The heavy scarf at Darcy's neck draped down the front of her coat, and she wore a hood and gloves and boots so the only exposed skin was on her face, yet the cold air fogged her breath to the point viewers couldn't clearly make out her features.

From the advisory, it didn't appear Emma or any of the other passengers diverted from Denver to Portal were going anywhere anytime soon. Figured. At least the plane had landed before the airport shut down.

Emma had been exhausted before getting on the plane, though the adrenaline rush had gotten her this far on the long flight. When taxiing in, she had spotted a hotel attached to the last terminal by a long breezeway, but odds were it was already booked or there wouldn't be so many people staking out sections of floor in the airport terminal itself. Every seat was taken and most of the floor, too.

She searched her jacket pockets. Found her phone and half a tin of cinnamon Altoids. No purse, no money, nothing but the clothes on her back and the ticket and ID she'd had the foresight to stash in her slacks' pocket before making the rescue attempt. Darcy Keller had been right. It was going to be a rough couple of days.

Emma walked on from the gate area, looking for a less populated spot with at least semi-privacy to phone in a report to Home Base. The second terminal was as crowded as the third had been, and the first, Terminal A, was even worse than B or C. The din of voices droned a constant hum that hung in the air. She pressed on to the northern end of an area identified by signs as "the Main." It was a broad and expansive opening defined by overhead, tented awnings, a food court and clusters of shops. Midway through it, she spotted a blessedly empty alcove and ducked into it, then retrieved her phone and contacted Home Base.

"Silencers. Liz speaking. How may I direct your call?"

Seeing the young redhead in her mind, Emma spoke softly. "Liz, it's Emma." Why was the Director of Operations answering the phone rather than the receptionist, Billie?

"Are you on the ground?"

"Yes, but not in Denver."

"They diverted you to Portal, correct?"

"Yes. And as soon as we were wheels down and landed, they shut the airport." Emma scanned the crowd rushing the food court. "Any chance you can get me some transportation out of—"

"None," Liz said, cutting her off. "You've been diverted."

Spotting an older silver-haired man with a thick briefcase and stooped shoulders, Emma visually followed him from an outlying sportswear store to the food court. Definitely browsing. "We've established that, Liz."

"I don't mean the flight. I mean, we—Silencers—have diverted you."

Surprise streaked through Emma. They were reassigning her to another security detail assignment already? She hadn't yet gotten home from the last one, and it had been grueling. Hostage rescue operations were always rough. "To where?"

"You're there. Portal International Airport."

"Seriously?" More perplexed than anything else, Emma inhaled deeply and caught the scent of lemon. She looked up and sure enough, there was a vent overhead. Why anyone, especially in an airport, would mask scents, she had no idea. It was a prime violation of protocol and an opportunity for unsavory types to insert bio-contaminates.

"Seriously," Liz said. "Look at it this way. You're stuck there anyway. At least you'll be busy during the storm."

"There are thousands of people crammed into this facility, Liz. Surely PIA has its own security team." Every international airport did these days.

"It does," she agreed. "But your assignment isn't to secure the facility or the people."

That disclosure made Emma's mission as clear as mud. Briefcase Man reappeared with coffee and a pretzel. "What am I securing then?" Emma couldn't imagine.

"Just let me tell you, okay? I'm slammed here today—

3

Billie is out until God knows when with the flu—so I need to streamline for efficiency."

Emma didn't sigh. She wanted to, but she didn't. "Fine. Go ahead."

"Use your same cover. Investigative journalist for American National Reporters—and no Loeb Award nominations this time. The director is still freaking out over the notoriety on your first mission."

Emma nearly had been booted from Silencers' training program over that. Security Specialists were most effective if forgettable and unnoticed. According to Liz, Emma's looks were Strike One against her. The award nomination, a huge Strike Two. If she got a Third Strike, she would be kicked out of the program. It was that simple. Everything she'd been working toward these past three years would be gone in a snap. No discussion. No reprieve. And no exceptions. Her fingers curled tightly around the phone. "I understand."

"Stay put under the tent in The Main. That's an area with stretched canvas overhead in the main terminal."

She'd seen the signs. "I'm there now."

"Good." Liz sounded relieved further explanation was unnecessary. "Apparently, a lot of construction's going on there."

"Noted that on the way in. Looks especially comprehensive on Levels Three and Four."

"It is, or so we're told. Heavy renovations. Fortunately, you'll be located elsewhere in the facility, so it shouldn't be an issue."

Regardless of where you were located in the facility, those open construction areas created worrisome vulnerabilities. Emma refrained from saying so.

"Your point of contact will retrieve you in fifteen minutes. Six-two, one-ninety, blue eyes, hasn't shaved in a few days, but he's a good-looking guy. His name is Dr. Gregory Martin."

Checking her watch beneath her black coat sleeve, Emma stilled. "Dr. Gregory Mason Martin?" Her throat thick, she waited for Liz's response. Dread churned with curiosity in her stomach.

"Yes, that's him."

A shiver coursed up Emma's backbone. Of all the people in the world, why him? The entire mission just wrapped up had been like this. She hadn't been able to catch a break with both hands and a net.

"Bio-containment expert. He runs the high-containment facility there that only a few know exists."

Emma frowned into her phone. "There's a high-containment lab here, in this airport?" What genius did that? Airports being terrorist targets had required they be hardened, but, good grief. Bio-contaminates in an airport? That was just insane.

"Afraid so."

Stranded in a wicked storm in a facility under heavy construction. Five thousand souls at stake, and now this. Bio-contaminates *and* Mason Martin. The news tumbled straight through bad and into worse. If not to protect the facility or people, why was she being diverted? "What's my job here?"

"Keep the lab secure," Liz said, then dropped her voice. "You know this doctor, correct?"

Another shiver coursed through Emma. "I do, yes."

"From a prior mission?" Liz asked, though she knew the answer already. Liz never asked a question she couldn't already answer.

"Actually, no. We grew up together and went to the same college. He knows me, Liz. My cover isn't going—"

"It will hold as much as is needed. His headquarters will see to it. This acquaintance could be helpful. If the doctor knows you, he is less apt to expose you."

"That's an assumption." Emma frowned. "He may be more apt."

"Oh, boy."

"What?" The scent changed to cinnamon rolls. She sniffed. Coming from the vent.

"That change in your tone. I only hear it when something is personal." Liz hesitated but when Emma remained silent, she added, "Were you engaged to him?"

Naturally, that'd be the first thing to occur to Liz. "No."

"Ah, so he must be the one who got away."

Surprise rippled across Emma's chest. "How do you know one got away?"

"Reasonable deduction. Anytime we talk about relationships, it's written all over your face," Liz said. "More accurately, it appears whenever we talk about the breakup of another of your relationships."

Emma clamped her jaw shut. Okay, so she'd been engaged a few times and had never made it to the altar. So what? Wasn't that better than a string of divorces? She opened her mouth to fire back a snarky retort, but fortunately good sense intervened. If she wanted to get out of training and off probation and be permanently hired at Silencers, Inc., the last thing she needed to do was to cross Liz and lose her support. "No, he isn't the one who got away." Oh, Emma hated admitting this. "Speaking honestly, he's the one I never got."

"I see." Liz's tone held empathy, proving she did see. Too much. "Well, hope springs eternal."

That remark pricked deep enough to obliterate Emma's restraint. "Shut up, Liz."

"Ooh, Touchy." Liz sounded amused. "Significant sign."

Emma couldn't deny it. She was touchy about Mason. She always had been. "I'm sorry. Habitual response. He's totally insignificant to me now," she reminded herself as much as Liz. "All that happened a long time ago."

"Evidently, not long ago enough."

Emma bristled, stuffed her free hand deeper into her black jacket's pocket. "Excuse me?"

"The wound is still wide open, Em. It's in your voice."

Was it? Probably was. She denied it anyway. "It's not."

"It is. It's evident," Liz insisted. "But let's don't waste time arguing the point. Either way, never kick an opportunity to the curb. That door is opening again for a reason."

"Yeah, right." Emma rolled her eyes back in her head, stared at the white ceiling, blanking out old memories she thought she had forgotten. "He's probably married with a couple of kids by now."

"Mmm, maybe. Want me to take a look?"

"No!" Emma cringed at having elevated her voice and then lowered it. Fortunately, others hadn't crowded into the alcove, so no one had overheard her. "No, I do not." Liz bent the odd rule when it was essential to mission success, but to violate his privacy on a personal interest? That was unexpected. So was the temptation to let Liz look. Not that Emma would give in to it.

"Okay, then." Liz sounded unaffected, as if the offer had been a test. "Well, if you change your mind…"

Definitely a test. Thankful Emma had tamped curiosity and refused, she assured Liz, "I won't."

"Fine. But if you do—"

"I won't, Liz." Emma sniffed. "Some opportunities need to be kicked to the curb and some doors are best left shut."

CHAPTER TWO

Emma saw Mason weaving through the crowd. Her breath hitched and she gave herself a mental shake. He was no longer lanky, instead he was muscular. His face was more angular, and she liked the scruff of beard. It accentuated his high cheekbones and slim nose. Gorgeous, as always. Even as a gangly boy, his face had hinted at the man he'd become. And the fitted blue shirt, cuffs still worn rolled up to just below the elbow, made his eyes appear all the bluer. Her breath threatened to hitch again, but the sudden downturn in his wide mouth into a formidable frown nixed that. He'd spotted her. And he was not pleased.

Mason intercepted her. "Tell me you aren't here waiting for me."

He smelled as good as he looked and sounded obnoxiously hopeful. "Hello, Mason."

"It's Gregory, as you well know, Emma." He didn't look flustered, just irritated. "Are you waiting for me?"

She smiled just to annoy him. "I am."

"Great." He shoved a hand into his slacks' pocket. "I need a security specialist and headquarters sends me a reporter. Batting a thousand today."

So was she; not that she'd mention it. She needed a battle with him about as much as she needed another close call on her life. "I'm glad to see you again, too." She sniffed and jutted her chin so he wouldn't miss it. Everyone else had called him Gregory or Greg. She'd only ever called him Mason, trying to get his attention. It had failed. But she kept up the practice to needle him. Compensation for his rejecting her.

"They honestly did send you?"

They, being his headquarters, of course. "I'm here. No one else is, or can get here," she said, lifting a hand. "So, do you want me to go or to stay?"

He didn't answer, but from his darting eyes, she saw the mental debate raging inside him. It annoyed her. "That was a rhetorical question, Mason." She folded her arms. "I'm staying."

His mouth twisted and a muscle in his cheek twitched. "Airport's closed. You're stuck. They're stuck. Now I'm stuck with a reporter when I need a security specialist." He sighed and engaged in a stare down.

Emma didn't flinch or flay him with a sharp comeback. She couldn't afford the luxury, being on probation. "For what it's worth, I'd prefer to be going home." That was the understatement of the year. It'd been six weeks since she'd left home on her last mission. "Blame your storm, not me."

His phone chirped, and he checked an incoming message. While reading it, the expression on his face went from irritation to surprise, then back to irritation.

Likely his headquarters was informing him of her arrival and position, as well as her security clearance. While she wasn't free to disclose her status outside of her cover, it was his headquarters' responsibility to assure that nothing impeded her work. How they'd pass off that work being done by a reporter was their problem, not hers.

Mason stowed the phone at his waist, then clamped his jaw. "You've been cleared. I don't get how, but my orders are explicit. Okay, fine. You're the boss. God, help us." He clamped his jaw. "Where's your luggage?"

"It didn't arrive." True, but not the truth. Still, he would believe it over the truth any day of the week. The ashes of her luggage were spread on a runway in Libya. Burned in a Humvee that came under fire seconds after she'd departed from it. She'd been lucky to escape with her life and the hostage she had been sent in to rescue.

A flash of movement over Mason's right shoulder caught her eye. A little girl about nine, wearing purple-framed glasses, a hot pink coat, teal neck scarf and a gray and white hat that was tugged down over her ears barreled toward him. "Incoming." Emma dipped her chin to signal him.

He turned and smiled, spread his arms wide. "Olivia." He swept the girl into a bear hug and straightened, lifting her. "I'm so glad you made it. We were getting worried about you guys."

Emma watched with interest. Obviously, he was fond of the girl and she of him. Was Olivia Mason's daughter?

She sneaked a look at Emma, then buried her face in Mason's neck. "Who is she?"

"She is my friend, Emma Miller," Mason told Olivia. "We grew up together. Emma is stuck here because of the storm."

The girl nodded. "Hi, Miss Emma."

"Hello, Olivia." Emma smiled. The girl was inquisitive, but Mason's explanation apparently satisfied her.

He didn't give her time to dwell on it. "Where's your mother and Jacob?"

Olivia pointed to an exotic looking woman with dark hair and huge eyes standing in a food court line with a little boy five or six. He held a stuffed beagle to his chest. "They're getting a cookie," Olivia said. "She promised Bandit one in the car, if he stopped barking."

"Bandit is Jacob's sidekick," Mason explained to Emma, while waving to the woman and the boy. "They go everywhere together and he's fond of chocolate chip cookies."

The woman and the boy waved back. Mason's wife and son? Emma had a hard time wrapping her mind around that. Her heart refused to accept it. Mason, married with two children, and he had been, apparently, for a decade. Something inside Emma twisted. Envy. Jealousy. Either or maybe both. And neither were welcome.

"Actually, Jacob is fond of all cookies." Olivia wrinkled her nose. "Bandit doesn't really eat them because he's stuffed. He doesn't really bark, either. Jacob does it." She dropped her voice to a conspiratorial whisper. "He thinks Mom doesn't know."

"I see." Adorably talkative and honest. Emma withheld a smile, but she had to work at it. "They're lucky to have each other, then."

"Well, I'm glad you're here." Mason set Olivia onto her feet on the floor. "You'd better get back over to them or you won't get a cookie." He smiled. "I'll see you guys downstairs in a few minutes."

Olivia nodded, quickly said, "Bye, Miss Emma," and then ran toward her mother.

Mason watched until she arrived at her mother's side and the woman smiled at him, acknowledging her awareness her daughter was back with her. He turned to Emma and all signs of warmth in him vanished. "Let's go."

Presuming they were heading to his lab, Emma stepped to his side and they walked. "You have a lovely family, Mason," she said.

"Sophia is married to my lab assistant, David Johnson. Olivia and Jacob are their children."

"Oh," Emma said, suddenly feeling light and not at all happy about it. Whether or not he had a family shouldn't matter to her. It shouldn't, and yet it did. "I assumed they were your family."

"Why would you assume that?"

Why had she? "Your face lit up on seeing them." He was well acquainted with the family or he wouldn't have known Jacob's stuffed dog Bandit's name.

"We're close," he conceded. "The kids think of me as their uncle."

He was fond of them, and clearly, they were of him. Stepping around a group of college-aged students traveling together, she asked, "So why are they here?" Of all days to visit the airport, this had to be the worst. The news report warning people to hunker down replayed in Emma's mind.

"To ride out the storm in the lab." Mason sidestepped a teen couple dressed in black with matching tattoos on their forearms. Keri and Matt. Permanent tats they'd no doubt regret when they went their separate ways in life.

"To ride out the storm?" Emma grimaced. He was letting kids into a high-containment lab to ride out a storm? What was he thinking?

"Their dad is here," Mason said. "Holly's not playing around. We could all be stuck here for an extended period of time. It seemed prudent to keep the family together."

"In a high-containment lab?" He couldn't be serious.

"In this one, yes." He pointed across the Main to the far wall. "Elevator's over there."

"In that hallway?"

13

Mason nodded and kept walking.

Emma followed, hoping she didn't have to report him.

CHAPTER THREE

Tuesday, December 17th
 1500 (3:10 PM)

THE PRIVATE ACCESS Only hallway dead-ended in a square room. An industrial elevator took up the entire far wall. Mason and Emma walked over then stepped inside. Its wide horizontal door made of thick steel slats slid closed. He pushed a raised red square button on the control panel, and Emma grabbed hold of a metal handrail and held on. The elevator lurched, then began a surprisingly smooth descent that seemed to go on for a long time before it finally stopped.

"How many levels are below the ground floor?" she asked, waiting for the door to open.

"Four," Mason said. "Plus, what we call the subterranean level. That's where the lab is located." From inside his shirt, he pulled out an ID card attached to a lanyard then held it up to a circular scanner embedded in the control panel.

The door groaned and then slid open.

Emma's stomach did a little flip. Rather than the light and

bright colors used upstairs, everything down here was a muddy brown except the concrete floors. They stepped out and she scanned the immediate area. Abandoned luggage conveyers created a maze, motorized carts and trucks lined up, some occupied and running and others empty and parked. Heavy equipment was strewn all over the place, tall metal stairs, trucks with canvas sides and forklifts, and large sections of floor were roped off with black tarps that concealed the contents of whatever stood stashed behind them. Fumes from the running motors left a noxious scent lingering in the air that burned her nose and stung her eyes.

"Shouldn't the luggage carriers be full?" she asked. "There are five-thousand stranded passengers upstairs."

"These are off-limits for facility use because of the lab."

"Ah, I see." Logical to minimize traffic in the vicinity.

"This way," Mason said, leading her to a long row of what looked like numbered golf carts. At 47, he stopped. "Our ride."

Emma got in and Mason took off with authority. She grabbed the side of a roll-bar. "It looks like a cart, but it moves like a Humvee. How fast does this thing go?"

"I'm not sure," he said, pulling to a stop in a line of vehicles waiting to enter a tunnel.

Shortly, they were inside the tunnel, and traffic moved at a slow but steady clip. At a fork, where the one tunnel split into two, most of the vehicles turned off. Mason sped up and pressed on, zipping through countless twists and turns.

"That question about speed wasn't a challenge." Odd murals on the walls snagged her attention. They were dark, of groups of people in pain and suffering. Fire and sparks, smoke and horrific images that burned a sense of desolation and despair into her mind. "This place is creepy." She glanced over at him. That he didn't seem troubled by them surprised her.

"They are supposed to be, to discourage people from

coming down here," he said. "Put your blinders on. That's what I do every time I come in or go out."

"It's like a whole city down here." One with so many tunnels splitting off into others, she was losing her sense of direction. "How many tunnels are there?"

"I don't know how many. About 17,000 feet of them all together." He gripped the wheel and shifted on his seat. "People get lost down below all the time."

"Down below. Street level?" she asked.

Mason nodded.

"I'm confused. How do unauthorized people get down here to get lost? It's a restricted area." She frowned. "You had to scan your ID to get off the elevator."

"Observant."

She shrugged. "Part of my job."

"Some of the tunnels on the uppermost lower-level are open to the public. There are offices and coffee shops, fast food places and that kind of thing. It saves the people who work down here from having to go above ground for everything."

"So, passengers wander from the unrestricted areas into the restricted ones?" That was not good news.

"It's a little more complicated than that. Only a couple hundred feet of all the tunnels are unrestricted. Just on the first of the four levels below street level." He shrugged. "Occasionally, there's a curious gawker. Not often. But some do get lost and wind up in restricted areas. Not so much on the subterranean level near the lab. It's much more isolated."

The floors of their current tunnel were painted with bizarre creatures. Ones long since extinct, and others that were pure fantasy and conjured right out of some troubled mind's nightmares. "Seventeen thousand feet of tunnels," she said. Impossible for one person to guard, and a challenge for one security team to fully monitor. "Does all this mean the secret military facility conspiracy theory is true? Is there one on the premises?"

"Not here," he said. "At least, not that I've seen. No aliens, either." He glanced her way. "That disappoints often."

"With a name like Portal, I can see that it would."

"Of course, I haven't explored all the tunnels, so who really knows what's down here?" He looked in her general direction. "My job is the lab. I focus everything on it. The rest I leave to the facility security chief and his team."

Ahead, the overhead lights were off, or they didn't exist. From her position, it appeared to be a dead-end. Mason drove on, never reducing his speed or tapping the brake, so apparently that dead-end wasn't one. It didn't raise any alarm in him. The cart plunged through the mirage of wall and into pitch-black darkness. "Slow down, Mason."

He didn't, but he did turn on the cart's lights. Only the right one worked, and it barely penetrated the inky-black darkness. A still silence fell in the tunnel and the absence of light made it feel close and cloying. Instinctively, she drew in a deep breath.

"Hold on," Mason said. "We're almost there."

Couldn't be soon enough. She'd never before been claustrophobic. No light. Sudden temperature change. Still air. The combination had triggered the sensation. Knowing it, she put it out of her mind and breathed normally.

About a hundred yards into the darkness, he suddenly stopped.

"Is something wrong?" she asked.

"No. Why?"

"There's nothing here, Mason."

He pointed to the left wall. Though dim, the light from the cart revealed a sign painted on it, like the murals. It read: *Authorized Personnel Only. All Violators will be Prosecuted.*

He got out of the cart. So did she, and she then walked

around the rear of the cart to his side. Only then did she see the outline of a door painted the same muddy brown as the walls. Even the doorknob was the same dull and drab color. If he hadn't stopped right in front of it, Emma never would have seen it.

"This is the entrance to the lab." Mason pressed his ID to the wall on the left side of the door. "Not much to look at, but we don't get visitors."

"I'm going to need an ID so I can come and go," she said. "I hope you never need an ambulance. I doubt EMT could find you."

"I couldn't call them anyway," he said, reaching for the door knob.

"I see why you don't get much of the lost traffic. If anyone makes it through the murals and creatures painted on the floor, they're fooled by the fake dead-end or far too tense to risk the darkness."

"Accurate assumption, I'd say. It's been effective. That much, I know." He almost smiled. "See? There is a method to the madness."

"It appears there is." She'd give him that one. "Most of the ride was downhill, correct?" When he nodded, she added, "It's hard to be sure, with the downhill slope and all the curves and turns, but I'm guessing we're three levels below ground here."

"That's correct, yes."

"I thought you said it was four."

"I said there are four levels below ground, plus the subterranean level."

"The subterranean level is where the lab is, right? That's where we are now."

"I didn't say where we are now."

"Sly." Okay. They were three levels down. That made her a little nervous. For deadly pathogen storage, three levels didn't seem nearly enough, especially not with a busy airport above.

"We're inside a mountain, Emma. They're not symmetrical. Some areas are four plus, some are three and some are one."

"I get it." In this area, the third level below ground was the subterranean level.

He opened the door. Light flooded out into the tunnel. The sudden sense of someone watching them hit her hard. Emma spun and scanned the tunnel behind her, then checked it again one more time. Nothing in sight beyond a maze of more and more tunnels. Yet something had triggered her senses.

Probably the creepy murals and floor art...and being this close to Mason again.

The sense of rejection she'd felt back during their college days hit her hard. Emma stiffencd, shunning the awful feelings of being measured and found lacking. That horrible feeling of caring so much about someone who cared absolutely nothing about you.

She gave herself a serious mental shake and a warning. Forget the past. Just forget it.

Even as she warned herself, she knew it wasn't the last time memories from the past would rise up and bite her. Next time, she would be ready and nix them the moment they started surfacing.

One thing was certain. Darcy Keller had been right. Between Holly and Mason, it was going to be a long couple of days...

CHAPTER FOUR

TUESDAY, **December 17**th
   1520 (3:20 PM)

BEYOND THE OUTER DOOR, Emma recognized the lab's layout. A contained area within a contained area. In the spacious outer ring were two offices and multiple doors. At a break in the solid wall, a hallway revealed four more doors and a wide opening into a common room. Glimpses of furnishings identified that room as a kitchen and living room combo. Sofa, bar-stools, a television.

With one exception, all the doors appeared to be constructed from regular steel. The odd door was a biometric vault door. That one, Emma felt certain, led to the inner ring, the high-containment lab.

She removed her coat, hooked it next to two others already hanging on a rack near the outer door. "It's warm down here."

Mason seemed surprised by the comment. "Do I really

need to explain geo-thermal—never mind. The outer ring in the lab is a constant 62 degrees."

"That's warm for specimens, isn't it?" Emma knew it was but asked anyway.

"Definitely," Mason confirmed. "Freezers containing the specimens are in the inner ring's HC vault. It's sealed."

HC. High containment. "I'll need the tour," she said, seeing a man about Mason's age leaving his office to join them in the outer ring. Unlike Mason, the man wore teal scrubs and a white medical jacket. He also wore clear protective eyewear and Poly boots for splash protection, which struck her as odd since he'd been in his office and not in the HC lab.

"David Johnson," he said, extending his bare hand. His smile was warm and friendly.

She shook his hand. "Emma Miller."

"Glad you got here," David added, releasing her hand and stepping back. "I feel better riding out Holly with a security specialist on the premises."

"She isn't a security specialist," Mason said, his tone slightly edgy and sharp. "She's a reporter."

"What?" David frowned. His confusion settled into anxiety. "What is she doing here?"

"She's a sub for the security specialist who isn't coming," Mason said, disclosing maximum information in minimal words. "Headquarters gave Emma full authority."

David's anxiety deepened.

Mason wasn't happy about her being here, but what was wrong with him, telling David that? Did the man seriously intend to make her job more difficult, undermining her credibility and creating doubt in her abilities? Okay, so he surely had plenty of doubts, but he didn't have to poison the well. Debating on whether or not to report him, Emma ignored him and turned to David. "I met your daughter, Olivia, upstairs." Emma smiled. "She's adorable."

That brought back David's smile. "She's quite a girl. Helps ease the way for her mother and me with Jacob."

What exactly David meant by that, Emma wasn't sure. She held her silence, seeing if he would explain more on his own.

He didn't, but Mason did. "Jacob is as shy as Olivia is open. He relies on her to watch over and guide him."

"That, he does," David said. "Takes all his cues on how he should react to things from her. Always has."

Emma nodded. "He trusts his big sister." That told Emma a lot about the girl. "And, I expect, Bandit."

David relaxed. "Ah, you met Bandit, too."

"Not officially. But I saw him from a distance." Emma wrinkled her nose. "I got beaten out on an intro by chocolate chip cookies."

David laughed. "Don't take it personally. With Jacob, everything and everyone gets beaten out by cookies—chocolate chip or any other kind."

Mason's mouth flat-lined. Why? Emma had no idea. He really didn't want her here; that was clear enough. Tolerating her didn't sit well with him, especially since his headquarters had given her full authority over his lab. She supposed she could understand that, though it should have occurred to him that the honchos wouldn't give her full authority without good reason. If his own bias against her weren't clouding his thinking, he would grasp that fact.

A low-level alarm sounded. Emma's gaze darted to Mason. No attention diversion. No signs of anxiety or focus shift. He wasn't concerned, so she held her silence.

"Ah, good. They're here." David started toward the outer door.

Obviously, the alarm was a warning, but only one signaling his family had arrived.

There were times when Emma's background in Criminal

Justice and certification in Behavioral Forensics came in handy. Of course, once she received the certification, it was considered a master's degree. Difficult program but it had provided extremely helpful insights into both criminals and victims. Now, in colleagues, too. Completing the program while working full-time had nearly done Emma in, but it'd been worth every night of lost or no sleep and scrimping and saving to pay for it.

"He's a happily married man. Stop trying to charm him." Mason grunted.

"I wasn't trying to charm anyone." Emma bristled. What was wrong with Mason? "I was just being civil." Dropping her voice so only he could hear, she added, "Maybe you should try it. Civility, I mean." Charm was too far out of his bailiwick.

That comment didn't win her any points. The muscle next to his eye ticked. It had always signaled his irritation. Seeing it, she didn't feel generous on letting his attitude pass unchallenged.

David introduced Emma to his family. Sophia was even more beautiful up close, and Jacob stared at the ground. Rather than speaking to him, Emma said, "Well, hello, Bandit." Then, she looked at Jacob. "May I pet him?"

Jacob darted a look at Olivia who nodded. "Okay," Jacob said. "But be gentle."

"Absolutely." Emma gave the puppy's ears a light scratch.

Jacob almost met her eyes. "He likes getting rubbed right between his eyes."

"Like this?" She dragged her fingertips lightly across the bridge between them.

"Uh-huh." Jacob looked right at her. "That's the only place he can't reach. Olivia says, no dog can reach there."

"Well, that makes sense, then," Emma said. "That he'd like that spot rubbed best."

Jacob nodded.

Sophia gave Emma a grateful look. "Let me get these two settled in our quarters, and then I'll start us some dinner."

"Thank you, honey." David dropped a kiss to her temple.

"No problem." She slid Emma a conspiratorial look. "Self-preservation. We've eaten their cooking before. Not happening today. Not with this storm. We need comfort food that isn't scorched or torched."

"Sophia loves to cook, and she's great at it," Mason said, having heard every word. "Unfortunately, she's right about David and me being kitchen-challenged." He lifted a hand. "Ready for that facility...um, tour?"

His hesitation was a message to her that he knew exactly what she was doing, pulling an inspection. He was confused by that, but he'd softened his verbiage anyway. She suspected, not for her benefit but for David's family's. "Ready. Yes, thank you."

David grabbed his family's bags and headed down the hallway after the kids. Sophia led the way. She knew exactly where she was going. Clearly, this wasn't the first time she and the kids had stayed in the lab.

David came right back and then turned toward his office. "I'm running a second safety check to verify we're ready for the storm."

"Better hurry," Mason told him. "Holly's barreling this way."

"You're certain to lose power, David," Emma warned him. He needed to include that in his systems check.

"Maybe up above but not down here," Mason told her. "Backup generators."

Of course. "Best check those then."

Mason lifted a hand. "They're not located on the premises. They're at the Armory."

"What?" That set off a warning in Emma. "All backup

systems deemed critical are required to be located at the facility."

"In this case—airport above, lab carved out of mountain —the honchos have deemed it safer to have power backup located off-site."

Emma would like to argue, but the odds of an airport being attacked were substantially higher than most other places on the planet, so she didn't. "Where is this Armory?"

"About thirty miles from here." Mason tried to reassure her. "Don't worry. It's a top-grade military facility."

Top-grade? After sequestration? That was highly unlikely. Facilities were in the process of being restored, but few were top-grade as of yet.

"The generators are up and running—David will verify that—and they haven't gone down once in five years."

"I'll check them," David said, quickly escaping to his office.

He had certainly picked up on the tension between Mason and her. Why was the man bent on making her job more difficult? David wanted no part of any conflict and proved it, bailing and leaving it to Mason to deal with her. She couldn't blame him for that. Either way David went, he lost. Emma withheld a sigh. "Before the tour, I need to make a call."

"Sorry," Mason said. "Phones don't work well in the lab."

"No problem." She moved toward the outer door. "I have a special phone." Stepping out into the tunnel, she reminded him, "You'll need to let me back in."

"No problem," he said, though he looked as if he were considering keeping her locked out.

Frowning, Emma closed the door behind her, gave her eyes a second to adjust to the dim light, and then called Liz.

When she answered, Emma dove right into what she needed. "You'd better get me a blueprint of this place and a schematic on its systems. Especially electrical." If the power went out, she could need them. "I'll need them for The Armory, too."

"Either or both?"

Be safe. "Both." Emma heard a rustling noise, retrieved her flashlight from her pocket, then shone the light beyond the two parked carts down the tunnel. Empty. "Mason says the Armory is about thirty miles away and the lab's backup generators are located there."

"Why?" Liz sounded as baffled as Emma had been.

"The honchos deemed it safer," Emma said. "All I can figure is for ventilation. Mason didn't object to the "safer" call, but I'm wondering. What could be safer than a hollowed hole in a mountain?"

"Located it," Liz said. "The Armory is about thirty miles, but even if you need to get there, you'll never make it in these weather conditions."

Emma worried at her lower lip. "Do we have anyone who can?"

"Not in this storm."

"So, there's no one on that site?" How could he fail to mention that? Deliberately deceptive? She parked a hand on her hip. "Is that what you're telling me?"

"Emma, that entire facility closed in 1992."

It had been out of commission all these years and Mason had called it top-grade? Impossible man. Totally impossible. "Then who maintains the generators?"

"Looking..." A pause, then Liz disclosed her findings. "It's classified." She sighed. "I'll requisition monitoring from head-quarters. They can try getting someone to them. I'm asking them to also monitor that entire facility during the storm to make sure the backups don't go down."

No way Emma could trek thirty miles to do it herself. That truth did it. Emma dropped concern and slid headlong into full-fledged worry. "Liz, I don't need to tell you what happens to pathogens if they heat up."

"I know. They activate."

"Yes. Active pathogens have no bias. No mercy." Emma shivered. "They spread, and they kill."

"Highly contagious. I know," Liz said. "I'm on it." Her voice wasn't quite steady. "Complete your initial assessment and then let me know exactly what we're dealing with here."

She wanted to know the specific pathogens. So did Emma. "I will."

"Try not to worry, Em. I'll be persuasive with headquarters." Liz hung up the phone.

Liz could be extremely persuasive, but even she couldn't dictate to Mother Nature. If they couldn't get to the Armory, odds were high that no one from headquarters could either.

Not worry? How could Emma not worry? She stood still, absorbed the gravity of her situation. An historical storm. Five thousand stranded passengers upstairs. A family taking refuge in a high-containment lab that wasn't supposed to exist but did, stocked to the rafters full of dangerous pathogens that if not kept frozen became highly contagious. And thirty miles of high power-outage risks between her and preserving those pathogens and keeping them frozen.

That recipe screamed potential pandemic disaster.

CHAPTER FIVE

Mason and Emma suited up in protective gear and then Mason opened the vault door. "It's okay," he said, picking up on her tension. "This is a decontamination chamber. The HC lab is still sealed on the other side of it. We go in, lock-down and decontaminate, and then enter the lab."

"Okay." She didn't mention she'd been trained for this and had successfully completed the simulator on it. Just stepped to his side. "Same process coming out?"

He nodded. "We lock-down, decontaminate, dispose of the suits in the chamber, and then exit. No problem."

She looked at him through the shield covering her face. "How do we dispose of the suits?"

"After decontamination, they're incinerated." He pointed to a chute in the wall. "Zero exposure to anything or anyone between here and there."

An air lock chamber separated the inner-ring—the high-containment lab—from the lab's outer ring and the rest of the facility. Leaving the decontaminate chamber and walking into the inner-ring's outer circle, Emma checked the negative pressure gauge—30, dead center of the -20 to -50 required. No dust streaks where the wall and ceiling met, so the seals were intact. She paused to check the electrical sockets. Intact.

"Everything okay so far?" he asked, sounding relaxed and at ease.

"Fine." She walked on, making the circle, examining everything she passed. Hands free, deep hand-washing sinks. Benches lining the walls were preformed and sealed. Floor was sealed concrete. No evidence of chipping or flaking. Chemicals and gases were minimal and stored appropriately. A minimum of cardboard and plastics, and it was substantially colder in here. "Below freezing?" she asked Mason.

"Thirty degrees."

Emma continued walking left around the circle. The safety-equipment area had fire extinguishers, a first aid kit, an eye washer. The fumigation valve and steel hoses met regulation standards. She spotted something unfamiliar. "What's that?"

"An autoclave. New to the market," he said. "It's a front loader."

"Total redesign," she said more to herself than to him.

A wrinkle formed in his forehead. "You're familiar with them?"

"Not with this model, no. But I am familiar with sterilization units used to purify waste before incineration. I did an investigative story on it a while back." She looked to the wall. "Microbiological safety cabinets." Emma turned to look at him. "How is air expelled in here?" The inner-mountain lab would require alternative methods. Scanning, she added, "Never mind. I see."

"What do you see?" Mason sounded curious, not suspicious.

"The air is filtered, oxygenated, and recycled." She peeked down at the regulators. All were well inside the green zone and spotless. She checked the tag. "PAT testing is current. Centrifuge maintained and serviced. Bucket seals are intact. Computers and their nodes are secure. And the bio samples are...where?"

He walked her around the circle to a tunnel on the far side of the decontamination chamber where they had entered. Inside it, crisscrossing light rays beamed, ceiling to floor. "Ionic?" she asked.

He nodded and they walked through the tunnel and into a separate work area that appeared to not have been used for some time. Upright freezers lined the wall. Appropriate glass fronts, and at the bottom of each was a written record, security-check sign-off form. All current and no blank lines.

"The pathogens," Mason said, motioning to the freezers with a gloved hand. "Each set of vials is clearly labeled. ACDP CL 3 Biological Agents Pathogens being used in an ACDP CL 3 facility are—"

It was a test. One she considered failing, but if he was to have confidence in her authority and his own headquarters, she had to pass. "Capable of causing severe disease in man that may spread to the community."

"In man or woman," he said.

"True. Gender isn't an issue with pathogens." They'd kill anyone. "So, nothing in here leaves here?"

"No. Nothing."

She walked down the length of the freezers, noting the specimen vials and their labels. Her skin crawled, and she recited the names aloud to help seal them into her memory for her report. "Tuberculosis, Cholera, Syphilis, Typhoid Fever, Tetanus." In the next freezer, she recited, "HIV,

Poliovirus, Hepatitis C, Small Pox, Cow Pox, Viral RNA Replication, Viral Oncogenesis, Herpesviruses, Murine Leukemia, Influenza, Dengue Virus." Her throat went thick. She swallowed hard and walked on to freezer number three. "Plague, BP7PP." BP7PP...? She scoured her memory but didn't recall ever seeing or hearing about BP7PP.

"You have Small Pox," she said, for the moment, skirting her obvious question about the strange virus. "Why? I thought it had been eradicated."

Mason nodded. "Yeah, well, things changed back in 2009."

She'd heard nothing about this. "What changed exactly?"

"We received highly credible intel warning us the Soviets were weaponizing it. We reacted to the threat."

A bio-arms race. She prayed it had been a micro-scale race and had quickly ended. "We reacted with what?"

"Actually, with BP7PP."

Tapped into the subject organically. Finally, she'd caught a break. "Which is what?"

Mason's expression sobered. "Black Plague—only much more deadly."

"More deadly?" Emma couldn't believe her ears. "Didn't the less deadly version kill 350 million people?"

"Between 350 and 450 million, I'm sorry to say."

Her skin crawled again, twice as fiercely as it had the first time. The truth dawned on her, and her throat went dust dry. "All of the specimens in here...they're all weaponized versions?"

Mason nodded, his expression behind his face shield grim. "I'm even sorrier to say, they are."

Emma swallowed a gasp and looked away. Heaven help them.

The risks she'd considered astronomical moments ago had just quadrupled.

CHAPTER SIX

Tuesday, December 17th
1700 (5:00 PM)

BACK IN THE OUTER RING, Mason smiled at Emma. "You look like you need a drink."

Finally, a smile. How could he be amused by her reaction to what was stored in the lab? There wasn't enough alcohol in the world to drink her way through this. Weaponized pathogens? Under an airport? "No, no drink. Facing this? Sobriety is definitely required."

He lifted a hand. "Coffee or tea, then?"

"Coffee would be good." She was chilled before learning that awful truth. Now the cold crept in deeper, freezing her bones. Maybe it was normal for him, but it wasn't normal for her. Especially not with Holly bearing down on them.

"This way." He led her through the outer ring and then down the hallway to the quarters section.

As they passed the second closed door, Emma heard

Sophia inside, playing a game with the kids. The constant thump of a ball hitting the concrete floor muted their voices.

"Olivia's practicing her dribbling. Basketball tryouts are right after the holidays. She's been at it since June," Mason said with a wry grin. "David says he hears the dribbling in his sleep. I bet Sophia does, too." He motioned to the end of the hallway. "The kitchen is right down here."

Emma's earlier glimpses of this area proved accurate. The end of the hallway opened into a large living room and kitchen combo. It shouldn't have surprised her to see the kitchen was well-equipped with a full-sized fridge, stove and two sitting areas. A table with six chairs and three stools at the breakfast bar. As much time as Mason spent here, he would have a functional and comfortable retreat. Long-ingrained habits didn't change. As kids, he'd created a similar space in their fort at home and often hid out there to read. He had loved his books. While Emma had read mysteries, Mason had read about germs and diseases. It hadn't seemed creepy then. It did today. Weaponized pathogens. As if the originals weren't horrific enough. "This looks like a normal kitchen." Emma sat down on one of the stools.

"It is a normal kitchen." Mason put on a fresh pot of coffee. "Obviously, I spend a lot of time here." He leaned a hip against the bar. "So, are you going to tell me how you know so much about high-containment labs?"

"I did tell you." She met his eyes easily. "I did an investigative report on them once."

"Missed that one." He filled the coffeepot with cold water. "When did you do it?"

"About two years ago," she said. The lie rolled easily off her tongue because it had been then when she'd done her training on them. It wasn't a lie really. Just a twist on the truth. She'd had to get used to those twists on her missions.

"I didn't see it."

"You mentioned that." His noting it twice raised a question in her mind. "Do you always watch to see what stories I have published?"

"Actually, yeah. I do."

That surprised her. "Why?"

"We share a long history, Emma. I'm interested." He walked back to the coffeepot, reached in the cabinet and pulled out two mugs. "You've done good work. No small thing, getting nominated for a Loeb award."

He knew about that, too? Well, that should help her on the credibility front, even if Liz would most definitely not approve and the Director would like it even less.

"You should have won."

"Thank you." His following her publications surprised her. Following her as closely as he had, stunned her. But supporting her for an award she could not win? Shocking. All this time, she'd believed he was uninterested and distant because that's all she had seen from him. But apparently that hadn't been all there was to it. He had monitored her through her work.

"I'd like to read it. Where can I find a copy?"

It would take time to digest that monitoring and to figure out why he had done it and what it meant. Yet he clearly wanted an answer to his question now. *Think, Emma. Think.* "Well, you can't," she said. "You didn't see the HC lab article because it wasn't published."

A furrow creased the skin between his brows. "Why not?"

"My editor was afraid it would incite too much fear in people." Emma shrugged. "To be honest, I think some politician nixed it, but that's just a guess." She frowned. "Fear sells. The honchos push for it and for the sensational."

"Unless they're persuaded to avoid it by those who prefer

any discussion stay off the public's radar. Probably cited to bury the story for reasons of national security." He frowned at the mugs. "I hear you."

He heard her but he didn't believe her. She sensed it with every bone in her body. But, at least so far, he hadn't called her out on it. Few reporters would ever be granted access to an HC lab. Not unless they were owed a fistful of favors, and even then, a visit wouldn't be welcome. Would he call her out? Maybe. Maybe not, if she distracted him. At this point, that was about her best shot. If he didn't know her so well, this wouldn't be an issue. It hadn't been before. But he did know her well, and that complicated things. "Can you answer a question for me?"

"Still drink your coffee black?"

He'd noticed that, too? Not trusting herself to speak, she nodded.

He placed a mug of steaming hot coffee on the bar in front of her. "Shoot."

Still simmering inside, she asked, "What brain-dead jerk put a bio-weapons storage facility under an airport?"

"I don't know, but it's been here for years." With his mug, he walked around the bar and sat down on the barstool beside her. "Without incident."

"By the grace of God."

"Yes," he agreed. "And because so few people know it's here."

He had to get beyond thinking they were safe because so few knew about this facility. "That was once true. But it's not true now."

Skepticism riddled his face. "Why do you say that?"

"Mason, I'm here because someone knows who shouldn't."

"You aren't here because of the storm?" Suspicion now rippled off him in huge rolling waves, and he curled his fingers tightly around the handle of his mug.

"That, too." He needed to know the truth. About the contents of the text she'd received from Liz while waiting for him to retrieve her from the Main. "There's been a substantial amount of chatter. The Intelligence Community is...quite concerned."

"I'm aware of that. Headquarters gave me a heads' up before you arrived."

"Then you know the IC expects an attack on this facility."

"There's a remote possibility, headquarters said. There's always a remote possibility, but they said nothing about expecting an attack." He lifted his mug, sipped. "Come on, Emma. You've seen the facility now, and it's obvious you know what you're looking at. The lab is encased by mountain. How can anyone, even the most advanced group of terrorists, penetrate it?"

"Working on that. Still assessing vulnerabilities." Her emotions churning, she asked the question she'd wanted to ask since leaving the HC lab. "Mason, what happened to you?"

"Excuse me?"

"Why are you working here?" Lifting her gaze from the bar, she met his eyes. "You were going to save the world. Find cures and treatments. What happened?"

"I am saving the world." He shifted on his stool. "I make sure people are protected from what's in here."

"Your lab isn't active." Risky, being this truthful, but instinct warned her, he would know her true thoughts either way. Better to be out front with them. "From what I observed, it hasn't been active for some time."

His expression went lax. "Okay, you're right. That's true. We have been on monitoring-only status for a while." That grated at him. "But it wasn't supposed to be like this."

Disturbed and irritated. That was a good sign of trust.

And discomfort. Regrettable, but she needed to know the real picture. "What was it supposed to be like?"

"When I accepted this job, I was supposed to be here for a year. The specimens were slated to be moved to a special lab."

"The CDC in Atlanta?" The Center for Disease Control would be the logical place for specimens, but did that include weaponized versions?

He avoided her eyes. "Close."

Silence stretched on between them. He had refused to disclose, and nothing she said would change his mind. She pulled back and tried an alternate route. "So, you've been here how long?"

"Five years."

She hadn't expected that. And now he knew she hadn't been monitoring him or his career. "Why weren't the specimens moved?"

"Budget issues." His voice went deadpan flat. As flat as the look in his eyes. "It was during sequestration. Budgets across the board were slashed to the bone, and what money was available was needed for other things." Clearly annoyed, he snagged his mug and refilled his cup. "More?" He lifted the pot.

She nodded and shoved her mug across the bar toward him.

As he poured, he went on. "We were at war, Emma. Still are. When you've got active mission planes robbing the boneyard for parts, there's no place left to siphon funds from, and everyone knows it."

"Budgets have been replenished now."

"Some have, yes, including ours." He returned the pot to the warming plate, then reclaimed his seat. "We were finally set to make the move next week, but then Holly came up. Bad timing for a bad storm."

"Word on the move leaked," Emma guessed. "That's what spurred the chatter."

"Probably," he said. "But no leak originated here."

"How do you know that?"

"Only David and I are here. I didn't leak, and if he had, he certainly wouldn't have his family here now."

Logical. "The leak came from higher up, then," she said. "Who exactly do you work for?" Liz would have the information, but Emma asked the question anyway. She wasn't at all certain he would answer her.

"U.S. Army Medical Research Institute of Infectious Diseases," he said, then issued her a stern warning. "Do not write about that or about me. You'll get us both killed, and I'm not ready to die."

He wasn't exaggerating, he meant it. Not that she had needed the warning. He couldn't know that though, so she didn't mention it. "Neither am I. Nowhere near ready to die." She looked him right in the eye and spoke the unvarnished truth. "I have no intention of writing an article about any of this. I promise." Many around the globe would love to get their hands on Mason. Both for what he knew and for what he could do. That fired protective instincts in her she hadn't expected. Strong protective instincts that weren't entirely welcome but accepted.

The look in his eyes pierced her. "One day, I am going to ask you that question."

"About writing?"

"No," he said. "About who exactly you work for."

She stiffened.

"Relax, Emma. I'm not slow on the uptake. I won't ask today. But I will one day. Just giving you notice."

Promise or threat, either could end her probation and bounce her right out of the Silencers, Inc., program. The standing policy was she could tell one person the truth about that. Only one. Ever. She smiled. "One day, I could answer that question, but it would put me in the position of making a choice I know you don't want me to make."

"What choice is that?"

"If you ask and I answer, I'll have to marry you or kill you." She held her smile, proving she was up for either. "So I know...any preference?"

That knocked him on his heels. His jaw hung loose, and he just stared at her.

She hadn't seen Mason flabbergasted ever. Not even when they'd sneaked into Grouchy Green's orchard and had been caught red-handed plucking grapes off his vines. Emma laughed. "Don't worry, Mason. I won't answer your question today." She tilted her head. "In fact, I won't answer it until you ask me the question again. That's a promise."

"You still keep them?" he asked, a little crease forming on his forehead between his brows. "You used to, but—"

She lifted her right hand. "I never break a promise."

Relieved, he cleared his throat. "Fair enough."

Her phone pinged.

Mason swiveled to look at her. "Your phone works in here?"

"I told you it was special." Smiling, she slid off the bar stool and answered, walking down the hallway toward the outer door. "Miller."

"Emma," Liz said. "You all okay?"

"We're fine. Why?"

"I'm patching through a weather report. You need to watch it, Emma. Right away."

Emma stopped at the neck of the hall. "What's happened?"

"The airport has sustained some storm damage. Significant damage."

"Where?" They'd heard nothing. Mason hadn't been alerted to anything going on. Surely Security would have informed him of any problem.

"Portal. The airport you're in right now."

Emma squeezed her eyes shut for a brief second. "It's a huge airport. What area has been damaged?" Mason came down the hall, took one look at her face, and stopped.

"Street level. Way too close to you."

Mason asked, "What's wrong?"

"Watch the weather." Emma whispered. "Damage above. Street level."

"Emma, are you there?"

"Yes, I'm here, Liz." Every nerve in her body hit high-alert. "Have the tunnels been breached?"

"I can't tell from here. I need sensors. Any alarms there?"

"No, none."

"Reporters are now on the scene. Darcy something or the other."

"Keller. Darcy Keller," Emma said. "She's pregnant."

"How do you know that?" Liz asked.

"I saw her on a road-side weather report right after I landed."

Mason skirted around Emma and she followed him. "I'll watch. Anything else?"

"You make sure that lab stays secure."

Worried. And nothing Emma had to report on the specific pathogens would do a thing except jack-up that worry to terror. "So far, there's no sign of trouble in the lab." Emma checked to be sure Liz had called on a secure line. Verifying she had, Emma shared her report on the weaponized pathogens.

"But that's insane."

"My sentiments exactly." Glad they agreed, Emma went

on. "A direct impact of political sequestration on the real world." Emma frowned. "You getting reports of more chatter?"

"A lot of them."

"How solid are they?"

"Historically reliable."

That set Emma on edge. "In this case, that's not good news."

"No, I'm afraid it's not." Liz's voice tensed even more. "Emma, I know I ride you hard, but that's because you're good. You're really good. You can handle this."

She wished she felt as confident as Liz sounded. But how she felt didn't matter right now. She had a job to do. She had to keep the storm and the terrorists from killing them all, including themselves and her, if that proved possible. "Do you know who they are yet?"

"Not yet. We're winnowing down possibilities. My instincts are telling me it's a private group. They seem to not have a political agenda. All reports indicate they're in it for the money."

"Black-market sales?"

"That's what my gut says, based on what we know so far. But I could be wrong."

Unlikely. Liz's instincts were honed to a fine edge. Experience in her job made that unavoidable. It left no room for illusions but relied hard on facts. Otherwise, Liz would be dead. "For the record, when was the last time you were wrong?"

"You don't want me to answer that right now."

"It's been a while, though?"

"A long while, yeah."

"Are you wrong now?"

Liz hesitated a long moment, then answered. "No. No, I

don't think I am." A heavy sigh crackled through the phone. "The Director is summoning me," she said. "I swear, if Billie doesn't get over the flu and get back to work, I'm going to scream until they straitjacket me. Watch the weather report, Emma."

PORTAL 3 NEWS

A male anchor stood in the studio in front of an animated radar screen. "Residents are feeling the brunt of the storm in Portal. The temperature is now four below. Winds are steady at 78 miles per hour and gusting to 96. Folks, do not attempt to go outside. We have whiteout conditions, heavy snow and ice, and winds that equate to a Category Two Hurricane. Reports are flooding in from all over about power outages and falling trees. Authorities warn residents to avoid downed power lines and the risks of trees falling or being uprooted by high winds. Conditions are extremely dangerous. Unfortunately, they are still deteriorating. The weather is going to get even worse before it gets better."

"Sorry to interrupt, but we have breaking news from Darcy Keller, who is at PIA in Portal. Go ahead, Darcy."

Keller's image appeared on the screen, replacing that of the male anchor. She still wore her red coat, but she stood inside the airport. Gauging by the stretched canvas overhead and the cluster of shops behind her, she was in the Main. Briefcase Man stood in the crowd gathered to her left.

"The terminals are on lock-down," Darcy Keller said. "For

those viewers who may be unaware, Portal International Airport is currently undergoing extensive renovations. There's a lot of heavy equipment on the grounds outside and inside the facilities.

"About fifteen minutes ago, heavy wind gusts whipped nearly everything not nailed down into segments of the buildings. The short- and long-term parking area has cars that have haphazardly flipped and stacked. Many have sustained damage. From a visual, it's difficult to find a windshield that isn't cracked.

"Near one of the renovation sites outside Terminal C, two cranes that had been secured with steel cables broke free and somehow crashed through..."

The transmission froze.

The screen went black.

CHAPTER SEVEN

Standing in front of the seating area off the kitchen in the lab, Emma turned away from the blacked-out screen to Mason. "Where's Terminal C in relation to where we are now?" She'd only had time to glance at the plans Liz had forwarded, but the lab didn't appear to be on it.

Mason rubbed his neck. "Way too close," he told Emma. "Just on the other side of the lab, about four levels up."

"I thought you said we were three levels down."

"I did. And where we were standing, we were. But the HC lab and beyond it are four levels below street level."

"Okay." Emma frowned, promising herself she'd be annoyed later that he hadn't explained that the first time she had asked. "We need to assess the damage."

Alarm flashed across his face. "You're thinking the damage above might not be from the storm."

Astute, not that she expected anything less from Mason. "I don't know. That's why we need to assess it."

David rounded the corner. "Dr. M.," he addressed Mason. "John Taylor's just locked down the entire facility."

Emma blurted out, "Who—?"

Mason swiveled to look at her. "John Taylor Moore is the Security Chief."

"John Moore," Emma said, capturing it in her memory.

"He prefers John Taylor," Mason said. "John was his father."

"Noted." Emma nodded.

David went on. "Janette Wilson is fighting him on the order, causing trouble."

"Janette is the Assistant Airport Manager," Mason said before Emma could ask the question. "She causes everyone trouble." Mason then spoke to David. "Where's Graystone?" Before Emma even thought to ask about him, Mason told her, "Graystone is the Airport Manager."

"He's still in the hospital," David said, then informed Emma. "Graystone had major surgery yesterday." David stuffed a fisted hand into the pocket of his white lab-coat. "John Taylor says he needs you to pull rank on Janette—the sooner the better."

"I'm going to assess the damage," Emma said.

"Then come with me." Mason stood up.

An explosion rocked the air.

"Far side of the lab," Mason said in a rush. Eyes stretched wide, he grabbed Emma to steady her on her feet.

"Weapons?" she asked.

"It's an airport, Emma."

"I know that, Mason. Are you telling me this facility is so inept it has nothing with which to defend itself?"

"I didn't say that."

She glared at him. "Stop parsing words, like you did with

the below ground levels. I need weapons." Hers were in the ashes of her burned luggage on the airstrip in Libya.

"John Taylor is armed." Mason shot her an apologetic look. "I'm sorry. It's an ingrained habit."

She nodded, accepting his apology. "Let's go."

Mason headed for the cart, but Emma noted something coming toward them from the opposite end of the tunnel. "There's our problem." She pointed ahead to where smoke and ash lifted from the ground to the ceiling of the tunnel and obscured their view. "Cover your mouth and nose." She grabbed the edge of her scarf and wrapped it around her neck, then tucked it in at her nape. Mason did the same with his. Together, they ran toward the trouble.

Closing in on the dense cloud whipping past them, they slowed to make their way through crumbled rock and partially downed steel beams. Gritty debris filled the air and stung their skin.

"The wind down here is wicked," Mason said. "That's not a good sign."

It was a terrible sign. Frigid air gushed over them. Emma raised her voice to be clearly heard. "It's blowing hard through the tunnels, creating a Venturi effect." Moving down the tunnel was a struggle. At a vee, they turned. The winds weren't as strong here. For that, Emma was grateful.

Mason stumbled over something on the tunnel floor.

An unconscious man.

Emma dropped to her knees beside Mason. The prone man was covered with dust and his face was smudged with dirt, but there was no sign of blood. "Who is he?"

"John Taylor. The Security Chief."

CHAPTER EIGHT

Tuesday, December 17th
1830 (6:30 PM)

Mason checked for a pulse. "He's alive."

"I don't see any blood anywhere." That struck Emma as strange.

"Maybe debris got him."

Maybe it had. But he was too far from the nearest beam, and there were no large objects within the immediate area he'd fallen, and no scuff or drag marks in the dust, indicating he'd staggered and then fallen.

Mason frowned over at her. "Why are you patting him down?"

She retrieved John Taylor's weapon. A Glock. "Looking for this." She checked the magazine. Full and not recently fired. She tucked the weapon into her waistband and with her phone, began a video recording of the blast damage, certain it wasn't consistent with a couple cranes crashing through a tunnel. The dust cloud was less thick, but she pulled her scarf back up over her mouth and nose. "To penetrate this far underground, the blast had to be caused by explosives."

"What happened?" she heard Mason ask.

Glancing back at Mason, Emma breathed a sigh of relief. John Taylor had regained consciousness. She worked her way back to them in time to hear his response.

"Five men. Armed. All dressed in SWAT gear. They're inside, Doc."

Another explosion went off and the blast rolled down the tunnel in a dust filled cloud of smoke and rubble. Unable to do anything more than hunker down, they waited until the rumble ceased and the worst had passed.

"Everyone okay?" Emma asked.

"We're okay," Mason said.

"I'm fine, Doc. Just got the wind knocked out of me," John Taylor said. "Go help her." He half rolled and grabbed a rifle from underneath him. "Take this."

"I don't shoot," Mason said, hesitating.

"Give it to her, then."

"What makes you think she can shoot?"

"The way she handles a weapon." John Taylor grunted, pulling himself up to a sitting position. "I just need a minute. Sorry. Someone whacked me from behind."

"Figured," Mason said. "You've got a sizable goose egg on the back of your head."

John Taylor rubbed at his skull. "I saw stars, and my head's still swimming a little."

"You collect yourself," Mason said. "Get to the Emergency Response Coordinator as quick as you can to get your head checked out."

"Janette Wilson laid her off when Graystone got sick. Busted her on a no-notice inspection. She hasn't hired a replacement yet." John Taylor rubbed his head and winced.

Only that woman would pull such a stunt with a storm

coming. "Go to the lab, then. David will fix you up." Mason scoured the tunnel and saw a shadowy Emma ahead. He started after her.

A shot ricocheted off the tunnel wall near his head. A second one followed. He heard it, but it sounded further away. Instinctively, he ducked. He couldn't see a thing. Had Emma shot at him? "Don't shoot! It's me, Emma!"

She appeared from the shadows. Gun aimed. "You okay, Mason?"

"Since you shot at me and missed, yeah." He walked toward her, his hand extended. "Give me that gun."

She stood her ground. "I didn't shoot at you, and you are not getting this weapon."

"Either time?" He'd definitely heard gunshots.

"No." She rolled her gaze, spun and fired.

"What are you shooting at?" Mason held onto the rifle. "Did you hit something?"

Emma stilled, scanned the visible expanse. While she'd like for Mason to hush so she could better hear, she knew him too well to expect he would until she answered. "Yes, Mason, I did."

He frowned deeper. "I hope it wasn't one of the employees."

"Is there a reason an employee would try to shoot you?"

Mason stared as if dazed. "You've stopped someone from shooting at me?"

"Three times, so far." She wiggled her fingers. "Obviously, you still hate guns."

"Um, yeah. But I'm learning a new appreciation for them being helpful in bad situations." He lifted the rifle. "John Taylor thinks you know how to fire this."

"I do." She stowed the handgun in her waistband, then took the long gun from Mason's hands and inspected it. Remington 870. Standard law enforcement issue. "Take this."

She passed Mason the handgun. "It's a Glock 19. Fifteen shots. I've used three. Point it and pull the trigger." She shot him a hard look. "Don't let someone shoot you dead because you don't like guns, okay?"

"Okay." He sounded a bit bewildered and confused, but he took the weapon.

"Good. Keep your finger off the trigger until you intend to shoot." She spoke softly. When he nodded, she went on. "You stay here. I'm going to see where the others are."

"There are others?" Rattled. To the core.

Shock of sorts. He hadn't processed and internalized what he'd been told about the team earlier. Being shot at did rattle even seasoned professionals. It was an event far outside Mason's wheelhouse. "John Taylor said five," she reminded Mason, sticking to the bare facts.

That cured him from whatever mental hurdle had stymied him. He was all business now. "I'm coming with you."

It was faster to agree than to fight with him. "All right. But I don't have time to argue, Mason. If I tell you to jump, just do it. And keep up or I will leave you behind. There are a lot of potential victims in this place. I need to secure it as quickly as possible." She took off through the tunnel. "Stay behind me," she said without looking back.

Emma made a bend in the tunnel and fired three shots in rapid succession.

Three men hit the ground. All wearing SWAT gear.

"That's three," Mason said softly, his voice a blend of shock and awe. "John Taylor said there were five."

"That's four," she whispered back. "The one who first shot at you is behind us."

Another explosion rocked their feet. Mason stepped closer and wrapped around her to cover her. "They're really close to the lab, Emma."

Her face at his chest, she whispered. "The sound was different this time."

"What does that mean?"

"It's bad. Really bad." She started moving. "Hurry, Mason."

At the tip of the next bend, Emma stopped and clothes-lined her arm to stop Mason. She placed a fingertip over her mouth, warning him not to talk. Then she pointed to a man crouched low against the tunnel floor where it met the wall.

Mason studied the dim shadow of a man. "Lab wall."

She nodded. "We've got two minutes until he sets off another explosion."

"Is that C4?"

"I hope not." She lifted the rifle and took careful aim.

"Wait." Mason urgently whispered. "Emma, wait."

"What?"

Worry and fear flashed across his shadowed face. "If that's C4 and you miss...?"

"I don't miss, Mason." She aimed then fired.

The man fell and Mason watched him, transfixed, his jaw hanging loose. He looked at Emma as if to ask, *Who are you?*

Before he could utter a word, something rustling behind them signaled movement. Emma swiveled and drew down.

"Whoa! It's me. John Taylor." He raised his hands.

Emma lowered the barrel of her weapon.

"I've seen four," John Taylor said. "That's the fifth."

"You're sure that's all of them?" This didn't work for her. It'd been too easy. Too straightforward, unless they thought there would be no one armed at the airport. Or that Security would be so busy with the stranded passengers above ground, it wouldn't have time to worry about what was going on down below.

"There could be more," he said. "I saw five before I got

knocked out. But there's no reports from anyone on my team picking up more on the monitors."

"Stay here. Both of you," she said. "I'll be right back."

Emma walked over to the downed man, verified he was dead, and disarmed him. Then she examined the explosives.

"What is she doing, John Taylor?" Mason asked.

Squinting hard, John Taylor answered, a little awestruck. "She's disarming the charge."

Shock pumped through Mason's body and he started toward her. "Crazy woman is going to get herself killed."

John Taylor pulled Mason back. "Emma said to stay put. You interrupt her at the wrong time now and you could cause her to kill herself. Or all of us. Just stay put, Doc." John Taylor watched her work. "She knows what she's doing."

Also observing, Mason crossed his chest with his arms. "It appears she does."

"What exactly is her job?" John Taylor asked, his glasses smudged with dirt.

Mason looked him right in the eye. "She says she's a reporter."

"No way." Interest sparked in John Taylor's voice.

"She knows her way around my lab, too."

"You know that reporter bit isn't so, right?"

"Yes, I know."

"Okay then." John Taylor grunted. "Who sent her?"

"I thought, my boss." Mason rubbed at his chin. "Now, I'm not so sure he didn't get orders from higher up." The woman in question was now photographing the dead men. Checking their pockets and bags for anything of interest. "Why is she touching them?"

"You deal with deadly germs and you're upset because she's checking pockets and bags on corpses?"

"But why is she doing it?"

John Taylor shrugged. "I don't know her, so I don't know

why, Doc. But I do know she's following protocol. I can't tell you exactly what she is, but I can tell you she's a well-trained pro."

"Finding anything?" Mason called out.

"Precious little." She didn't sound happy about that. "John Taylor," Emma added, "you'd better get a team down here to protect this area and secure these bricks."

"Did she say bricks?" Mason asked. "I don't see any bricks."

John Taylor nodded. "Bricks of C4 explosives. Apparently, she's found more of them."

Emma called out. "That last explosion opened the mountain all the way up to the surface. Better secure the opening above so no one stumbles down the hole."

"Roger. You got that charge disarmed?" John Taylor shouted to her.

"Yeah." She looked back to them. "But don't get too close. You'll taint the evidence."

"Isn't that your job?" Mason asked.

"She's the boss. Isn't that what you said?"

Mason nodded. "What was it? The explosives, I mean."

"Classic bricks of C4 apparently." That had a wrinkle forming between John Taylor's eyebrows and him swiping at his glasses at the bridge of his nose. "Not the most efficient means of blasting through the mountain, but..."

Emma stood up and looked at John Taylor. "Make sure whoever you send for knows how to handle C4 and gunpowder and canon fuses. Looks like they had a backup plan in case they didn't get the desired results. They did drill a hole in the rock. It's about eighteen inches deep. So they weren't blathering idiots, just not up to what they should have been, attempting something like this. That's good news for us." She dusted her hands and started back toward Mason and John Taylor.

"She's definitely a pro," he whispered to Mason, then raised his voice to Emma. "Got it. I've summoned a team."

"Arm them, and get a man on that back wall," Mason said.

John Taylor sniffed. "That's done, too."

"Where's Janette?" Mason grimaced. "She was supposed to be down here."

"No. She's upstairs on the Main, under the tent with the press."

Mason lifted a finger. "Not a word of this gets out. Not a word."

"I'll vouch for me and my team," John Taylor said, "but not for Janette."

Mason frowned. "Why not?"

"She's got her eye on Graystone's job, Doc." John Taylor twisted to keep an eye on Emma. "He's not doing well. Looks like he might not be coming back, and Janette is bent on replacing him."

"Spare us all from that. I am sorry to hear that about Graystone," Mason said, pausing a long moment to think. "For now, don't tell Janette anything about this." Her ambition could override her sense in her quest for attention. To give John cover—he did answer to Janette—Mason added, "That's a direct order."

John Taylor smiled. "You got it, Doc."

Emma was on the phone. That stunned Mason. Now? Here? With a dead man near her feet? Who was she talking to now?

CHAPTER NINE

"IT WASN'T THE CRANES," Emma told Liz. "It was an attack."
The rear wall behind her, Emma stepped closer to the hole in
the outer wall. Cold air rushed in. She glanced back, making
sure Mason and John Taylor were still out of earshot. Judging
them a distant twenty feet away, she reported to Liz. "Five
spotted, five down."

"I'm assuming that was unavoidable."

"Totally." Emma brushed at the tip of her nose. "The
Security Chief was unconscious when we found him. He's
mobile now. One invader took three shots at Mason."

"So Mason shot that one?"

"No, he doesn't shoot. I dropped him." She checked over
her shoulder. Nothing but the sound of the wind rippling
down the hole. "I returned fire on three others. The fifth one
was about to ignite enough C4 to take out the mountain and
leave nothing of the lab but a crater." In that situation, the

blast could destroy the pathogens or spread the diseases all over. Probably a bit of both.

"So, you neutralized the threat?"

"I did."

"That's an appropriate response," Liz said, her tone neutral when they both knew it was anything but. "There could be others, Emma."

"I know. None spotted so far."

"On these type missions, there is always a backup team."

"Yes." Emma was as aware of that as anyone else in the field. "Guards posted, and security team is on alert." She slung the rifle's strap onto her shoulder. "The problem is, there's one of me and this is a big place."

"Exactly how big?"

"Five levels above ground, four—in places, three—levels underground and 17,000 feet of tunnels. I haven't been spared a moment for proper recon."

"Is the lab secure?"

"The detonated charges have taken out a lot of rock, but I don't see a breach. Lighting down here is weak at best, but the rear wall of the lab appears intact. Beyond the lab, toward the outside and above the tunnel, is now open all the way to ground level. There's about two feet of rock between the tunnel opening and the lab's rear wall. Cracks are evident, Liz." Emma worried. Her stomach did a little flip. "Concern about a Venturi effect is warranted. It was relatively light but evident in the tunnels—low-grade—and storm winds aren't yet at full strength. If they get much higher, the wind could exploit the cracks and break through the lab wall."

"What are you going to do about it?"

Emma had been weighing potential solutions on just that. "Options being limited, about all we can do is fill the cracks, and add a snow pack."

"Reasonable," Liz said. "I'll need photos to ID the

subjects of interest and whatever you got off them. Also, I need any footage of the scene. I'll get the gurus to do a damage assessment. If they have any brilliant ideas, I'll pass them on to you."

"All of that should be sitting in your in-box," Emma said. "I transmitted just before I called."

"Have you done a gut-check?"

Emma didn't hesitate to share her instinctive reactions. "A hotel connects to the airport, just beyond Terminal C. That's the logical place they would have been holed up, and below Terminal C, there's a couple hundred feet of unrestricted tunnels. That'd be their easiest and most direct access point. Passports and identification weren't on them, so they had to stash them somewhere. Our best bet is at the hotel."

Airport lockers were a possibility, of course, but as crowded as it was right now, lockers would be difficult to acquire. And there'd be too many eyes watching. "I recommend you cross-check the hotel security footage and compare it to the photos I sent," Emma continued. "The attack was well-coordinated and well-funded. They have top-notch equipment, and a lot of it. Their explosives expert wasn't great, but he was good enough to get the job done. If we hadn't been here, he would have. I seriously doubt they'd come in on this kind of operation with such a small footprint."

"In other words, you think there's more of them and they'll come after the lab again."

"Exactly." And that certainty had Emma praying to be ready on her end. "We're short on weapons, so we'll surely be out-gunned. The airport's director, Graystone, is in the hospital. He had an unrelated surgery yesterday. The second in command is after his job and media friendly. She isn't trusted. Mason pulled rank and ordered the Security Chief to not inform her of the attempted attack. National Security priority."

"Sounds wise, under the circumstances."

"I thought so, too," Emma agreed. Mason and John Taylor were speaking softly, and John Taylor relayed a few orders through a two-way radio.

"There's no way we can get back-up to you, Emma—personnel or supplies. The storm has everything grounded. Even emergency services have shut down."

She figured that. Still, hearing it put knots in her stomach. "We'll do all we can," Emma said, praying it'd be enough. "Let me know who these people are as soon as you pin them down. Everything you can get on them."

If she stood half a chance, she needed to know their identities and histories to know what they were capable of doing.

"From your visuals, any clue if they're foreign or domestic?" Liz asked.

"Could be either or both." Their mixed messages on uniforms, weapons and personal effects had no doubt been intentional. "No idea. I also suspect they have a safe-house nearby. Someone, somewhere to hand off the pathogens to for further distribution."

"In addition to the hotel."

"Yes."

"Seems prudent."

"No identification, passports, transportation tickets or receipts on any of them."

John Taylor and Mason walked over to her. "Just a second, Liz." She covered the receiver with her hand. "Don't touch anything but take a look at them," she said, nodding toward the bodies, "and see if you recognize anyone."

They went to look, and she continued talking to Liz.

When both returned to Emma, she asked, "Anything?"

Both men shook their heads, no, they didn't recognize any of them.

"It's a bust on the identities," she said into the phone, then ended the call and spoke to John Taylor. "There's no one on the hole yet. You need to get someone above so no one or nothing falls down here, accidentally or deliberately. It's open straight through from the street now."

"Radioed my men on that a bit ago. They've got the area sealed off. I'll get an eyes-on guard on it." John Taylor peered at her through his oval-shaped glasses, his dark brown hair standing on end and falling in clumps on his forehead. He motioned to the rifle, then the Glock. "Can I have one of those weapons back?"

She passed him the Glock. "We need a couple guards on this back wall."

"I'll take care of it." John Taylor nodded. "We should document the damage."

"I did," she said, knowing he'd watched her do it. He was asking for a copy without asking—a professional courtesy. "I'll send you what I've got, and you can see if you need anything further."

"Sounds good." After relaying his email, mobile and text information to her, John Taylor started back the way he'd come, already issuing orders on his radio. "I need a guard down here now. Come fast and come armed."

"Make sure he's trustworthy," Emma said.

"If he wasn't, he wouldn't work for me." John Taylor paused, looked back at Emma and sniffed. "I screen very carefully."

"Excellent." She looked at John Taylor's retreating back. "I need to run some recon. Can you stay until your guys get here?"

"I'm not going anywhere," he said, his jaw set. "Do what you need to do."

"Thanks." Emma turned to Mason. "I need to check the tunnels. See if I can identify their approach. I'll meet you back in the lab."

"Okay," Mason said, his voice a little unsteady. "David says everything is testing out okay, but I need to inspect the systems myself." Worry settled into his expression, lining his face. "But I don't like leaving you alone in the tunnels."

She didn't like sending him back to the lab on his own either. "I'll be fine. You let me know when you get to the lab, and make sure the pathogens are secure. Otherwise, whatever else we do will be futile."

Mason still looked torn. "If you're sure..."

"I am. No arguing with me, remember?"

"I remember. Okay, then." Mason touched her shoulder. "Be careful, Emma."

The concern in his eyes was genuine. Her heart skipped a little beat. "You, too."

He took a step, then glanced back at her. "One day, when I ask you who you work for, I'm going to ask you about all your special skills, too."

"But not today."

"No, not today." He swiped at the back of his neck. "Though I have to say, I'm glad you've got them."

"Today, so am I." Emma nodded to clear her mind of what could have happened if she hadn't. A shudder coursed through her entire body. "Get going now. We've got a lot to do, and we need to do it quickly."

Before the attacker's backup team activated...

CHAPTER TEN

TUESDAY, December 17th
1947 (7:47 PM)

EMMA MET Mason in the outer ring of the lab. "Everything okay?"

He looked as relieved to see her as she felt on seeing him. "Let's go to my office." He nodded toward the kids, who were taking turns dribbling a basketball along a fifteen-foot stretch between the outer door and the one to the vault. "Sophia's in the kitchen and David's at the computer in his office."

The TV was on and Janette Wilson was speaking to the media. To Darcy Keller, to be precise. "The outer perimeter of the main terminal has suffered minor damage," Janette said. "But it's nothing that affects the integrity of the facility's structure."

She sounded reassuring. Calm and in control. That told Emma, John Taylor's orders to his staff to keep her out of the need-to-know loop on the breach had been followed, which meant his men trusted him, and Janette wasn't checking out the damage on her own. Graystone, being more experienced, would have. Janette Wilson might want Graystone's job, and she might look the part, but she wasn't ready for his job. That said, at the moment, she was good for the 5,000 stranded passengers upstairs who had to be edgy and hanging onto her every word seeking reassurance.

Darcy turned the conversation to the weather. "Hail and blinding snow…"

While Janette looked as if she'd just stepped off the pages of a fashion magazine, Emma was splotched with dust and grime. Her black slacks and jacket hid a lot but streaks on her once-white blouse were unforgiving. She swiped at one, smearing it, and then focused on Mason.

He signaled her with a head tilt and then started walking toward his office. She followed him to it, and when she stepped inside, he closed the door to the hallway.

"I ran a full security sweep on the HC lab," he told Emma. "Everything appears intact. There's no evidence of broken seals or of the cracks in the rear wall actually penetrating through it into the lab."

"That's good news." Emma scanned his utilitarian office. There was nothing personal in it. Clear desktop, blank white walls, blank concrete floor. A computer terminal rested on a side desk. Its screen was black. Its CPU disconnected. "Do you actually work in here?" she asked, having a hard time reconciling this space with the Mason she had known growing up.

"Not much now." He smiled and sat down behind his desk. "I told you. We were geared up for the move."

"That's right." That made her feel a little better. It boggled her mind to picture Mason working long hours in such a sterile environment. Oh, it'd be functional, but there was nothing of him in it at all. He'd always been neck-deep in stacks of papers and open books. A clutter bug, yet somehow organized to him.

"Sit." He motioned to a straight-back visitor's chair. It looked unused, and likely had been in his time here. The lab didn't get visitors, he'd said. "Did you find any answers down tunnel?"

She had found nothing. Not a thing. "They didn't come in that way."

"You think they came in from the outside wall? Moved in as they blasted?"

"I don't know yet." She frowned and sat down in his visitor's chair, shoving the rifle stock slung over her shoulder out of the way. "That's unlikely though. In that kind of infiltration, they'd generally have at least one man already inside, positioned just beyond the blast zone."

Mason rocked back. His chair squeaked. "You're convinced they were professionals."

"Definitely." She worked a kink out of her shoulder. "An amateur wouldn't recognize half their equipment much less be able to use it." The explosives guy wasn't at the top of his game, but he was competent enough to get the job done. The charge wiring had been pretty rudimentary. His choices would not have been the first choices of someone really good with explosives.

Mason lifted a hand. "So, what do we do now?"

"I check out all the tunnels," she said. "I'm having John Taylor and his team review security footage to see if they spotted the entry. And specifically, the elevator, which would have biometric information on at least one of them."

"Why?" Mason asked, folding his hands atop his desk. "They're all dead."

"To crossmatch them, if possible. We need to know who

we're dealing with so we know their capabilities. Different groups, shall we say, have different strengths and weaknesses. We identify even one of them and associate them to a specific group, we'll better know what to expect from the rest of them, and what vulnerabilities of theirs to exploit."

"Sensible, but not urgent, since they're dead," he reiterated. "So why is this as significant as it would be if any had survived? You're as tense as before you killed them all."

She could answer that, but she'd rather not if she could avoid it. It hadn't yet occurred to him that the first wave of invaders was exactly that—the first wave. "Let's say, I want to make sure there are no more surprises." She shot him a loaded look.

"Oh, no. I know that look. It's not over." He rocked forward and clasped his folded hands atop the desk. "You think there are more of them."

Well, that didn't take long. He always had been too good at reading her and too quick at projecting and deducing the obvious. Emma didn't respond.

"You can speak freely in here. My office is sound-proof and white noise is on all the time to avoid any intercept attempts."

"What about your computer terminal?"

He smiled. "Well protected."

She smiled back. No computer with Internet access was ever well-protected, regardless of how secure it appeared to be. But it was totally disabled, so his false sense of security was justified. Truly, they should be fine. "Then let's say, as best I am able, I want to be sure there aren't any more surprises."

"But you do think there are more of them coming." He gently rocked, studying her. "I know you, Emma. I told you, I know that look."

"Okay. Your ears only." When he nodded, she added, "I'd be shocked if there aren't more of them."

"Because...?"

She squirmed on her seat. "It would be atypical."

The gravity of that disclosure wasn't lost on Mason. He stood up. "I know you started checking the tunnels, but we need to check them all."

"We do."

"Let's go then."

She walked with him toward the outer door, stopped when he paused to speak to David.

"Keep a sharp watch," Mason told him. "Anything comes up, you call me on the radio right way."

Mason looked at Emma. "Radios are more reliable than phones down here."

"Do you have a spare?" she asked. The rich scent of spicy spaghetti sauce wafted from the kitchen down the hallway. Her stomach growled. "I should preserve my phone."

"I do," Mason said. He went back to his office to retrieve one, then returned and passed it to her. "Channel is set. You're good to go." He also passed her a flashlight.

"Thanks." She clipped the radio to the waistband of her slacks, then slung the rifle's strap over her shoulder. "Let's move."

Flashlights on, they headed out into the tunnel, and she peered over at Mason. "On this end, I want to check the tunnels between here and the hotel first."

"You think they were at the hotel?"

"I don't know yet, Mason," she said. Liz hadn't yet reported back to her on the security footage from there, though she had secured it. "But it's the logical place to start. Out of sight, off the airport security cameras, a private place to stow their equipment and identifications, passports... It's logical they'd hideout there until they were ready to move."

Mason kept pace with her and with the intense flash-lights, they methodically swept the tunnel, ceiling to floor, left to right. "Look for scrape marks, footprints, scuffs. Anything to signal someone recently came through here."

"There's a lot of loose dust that wasn't here before the blast," Mason said. "And the wind is drafting this way."

It was. Which meant any evidence likely would be beneath the dust. She kept moving. "For someone out of your element, you're astute on what to observe."

"It's common sense."

"Not exactly," she countered. "But you do have an advantage. Your work requires you to look for anomalies. Your mind works that way. It has since we were kids."

"True." He accepted her opinion graciously. "So, when are you going to tell me you're not a reporter?" He stepped to her side, and his flashlight stilled. "You're an anomaly, too."

"Remember our marriage or death discussion?"

"I haven't forgotten, and I'm not going there. But I am wondering at what point you'll trust me enough to tell me the truth."

"I do trust you," she said, taking a second look at a smooth patch on the floor. It was nothing. "And I really am a reporter."

He grunted, exaggerated it to make sure she hadn't missed it. "Right."

"It's true. I am a reporter." She lifted a hand. "How can you doubt it? You knew I'd been nominated for Loeb Award."

"True." He frowned and paused a minute. "Okay, then. When are you going to tell me your primary job, because it sure isn't reporting or investigative journalism, which is what I thought it was until today?"

That comment earned him a sigh. For an astute man, a brilliant one in multiple areas, he wasn't faring well on a simple-logic level. That wasn't uncommon, unfortunately. Give a genius a complex pretzel and he or she would untwist it. But a simple one, and they got bogged down in unessential minutia. "You need to think, Mason. What did you request?"

"A security consultant."

"Well…?"

"So, you really are a security consultant?" Mason seemed a little surprised. "I mean, you do act like one, and you have the skills and knowledge but… you're Emma."

"What does that mean?"

"I guess, I'm surprised. That's all. Are you a security consultant? Seriously?"

"We'll see," she said.

His jaw snapped shut. "Diversionary tactics again?"

"Not really." She stopped sweeping the light and looked right at him. "If I fail here, no. I am not," she said. "If I succeed, then maybe. Either way, it's not something I'm at liberty to discuss." She dipped her chin. "You're treading awfully close to the 'who do you work for' question, and you know what that means."

"I haven't forgotten. The marriage or death bit." He swiped at his neck. "You're as secretive now as you were when you were a kid."

"I wasn't secretive." She returned to her sweeping with the flashlight, mostly to avoid watching him stare at her. "I tried everything in the world to get you to notice me, especially in college."

He harrumphed. "Oh, I noticed you."

"You did not." She spotted a fresh gouge mark on the wall, where it met the floor of the tunnel, examined and then deemed it insignificant. "You looked right through me as if I were standing in a different dimension."

"I noticed you," he insisted.

"You avoided me." Emma hated how hurt she sounded. At the time, it had hurt. Apparently, it still did. That surprised her, and yet it didn't.

"Of course, I avoided you." He stopped walking. "You went through guys like they were items on a buffet. Who in their right mind wants to fall for a woman like that?"

Emma couldn't believe her ears. Could he have noticed her but been protecting himself? It was possible, she supposed. "That's never been intentional on my part," she said. "They sought me out."

"Of course, they did. You were stunning and charming."

That comment shocked her silent. She couldn't wrap her head around it.

"And you went through them like they were nothing."

"That's rubbish," she countered, genuinely offended. "They were all something."

Mason twisted his mouth to the left, clamped his lips together. "Emma, you might be able to tell that to someone else, but I was there. The entire time we were in college, you never dated the same guy longer than two weeks. Not one time."

Her face burned. He had noticed or he couldn't know that. She'd love to deny it, claim he was wrong, but she couldn't. "True, but the reason wasn't because they were nothing. Of course, they were something. Every one of them."

Skeptical, Mason stopped and stared at her. "Why did you dump them then?"

A question she'd asked herself at least a million times. "They just weren't exactly right for me." She told Mason what she'd told herself. "But in the beginning, I thought every one of them had the potential to be right."

"Seriously?" Mason's skepticism deepened. "You've dated some bad guys, Emma."

"Not too bad." She hadn't. Well, some had been losers. But most had redeeming qualities...

"And some nut-jobs."

There had been one or two. She couldn't dispute that

72

either. But hindsight is always clearer. So is looking at other people from a distance. You don't get the whole picture. "They seemed okay at the time," she insisted. "Some just didn't wear well." He had her on this one, too. Because she agreed, she couldn't even really resent it. Not with a clear conscience. "Maybe I didn't want to be judgmental."

"Discernment isn't a flaw."

Now he was annoying her. "So, I gave them the benefit of doubt, but when I realized they were wrong for me, I ended it. How could that not be the right thing to do? A lot of them were really good guys, just not right for me."

Mason slid her a deadpan look. "Like I said. Buffet."

Her temper flared. "Shut up, Mason." She raised a warning finger. "You're quizzing me like I've committed some crime, but you're still solo, too. What are you doing wrong?"

"Nothing." His lips curved and his eyes mocked her. "I choose to be solo."

"So do I." She'd ended relationships. A lot of them. And a couple engagements. Those had been her call, and she'd made it.

"You haven't been solo since puberty."

Arrogant jerk. "And you know this how?"

No answer. That muscle ticked under his eye and his jaw was tight.

She resisted the urge to stalk off. To say things she knew she would later regret. Things she wouldn't be able to justify to herself much less to Liz. He sounded awfully sure of himself. Cocky, and certain he knew exactly what . . . The truth hit her hard. "You've been keeping tabs on me all this time. Following more than just my career."

Again, no answer.

"Admit it, Mason. I know I'm right. That muscle in your jaw is ticking double-time. It always did when you were guilty or in denial."

73

He sighed. "I don't keep tabs on you. Your mother and I talk now and then. That's all. It's no big deal."

Her mother? They stayed in touch? That was a huge deal. And the reason Emma knew it was huge happened to be simple. Neither of them ever had mentioned it to her. Not once. "Mom always did like you best."

He flashed her a grin. "She still does."

Emma rolled her eyes back in her head and returned to work. The last thing she wanted Mason to know was the reason she went through men like they were items on a buffet. It'd taken her a long time to figure it out herself. In fact, she still wasn't totally sure she was right.

Mason paused, gripped her arm and dropped his voice. "Shadow ahead. Fifteen feet. Floor."

Emma swept the area with the flashlight. "It's a person."

Together, they moved toward it. She spotted no movement at all. Heard no breathy sounds. "Hang back and alert me if you see or hear anything."

Mason was already scanning.

Near now, Emma crouched down. "It's a man wearing an airport security uniform. If he was armed, his weapon is gone."

Mason moved in a wide circle around her, checking high and low. Spotting nothing, he circled until he could see her face, then stopped. "Is he—"

Emma felt for a pulse. "He's dead."

Mason shuffled around to see the man's face.

"Recognize him?" Emma asked.

"I've seen him, but I don't know his name. He is on John Taylor's staff."

A tight spot formed in Emma's chest. Mason looked a little shell-shocked. She understood that. In his line of work, he didn't see many bodies close up. Had he ever seen one outside of a controlled environment?

"Mason." Emma kept her voice low, modulated, calm. "Mason?" When he looked at her, she said, "We need to let John Taylor know. Someone who is supposed to be somewhere isn't. You understand?"

"Yes." Mason collected himself. "Yes, I understand."

"Call John Taylor and get him down here."

CHAPTER ELEVEN

JOHN TAYLOR ARRIVED in a dust-spewing cart with "Security Chief" emblazoned on the door.

"Don't go further down the tunnel," Emma warned him. "It hasn't yet been cleared."

He got out of the cart and joined them, dropping to his haunches. "He's dead."

"I'm sorry," Mason said. "Yes. From the bruising, we think someone approached him from behind. Seems consistent with strangulation."

"Who is he, and where's he supposed to be?" Emma asked.

Mason frowned at her. "Give him a second."

"I might not have a second."

John Taylor cleared his throat. "Kyle Greer," he said, looking up at Emma. "He was supposed to be guarding the lab's rear wall."

He hadn't made it there or something had forced him to leave his post. "Was he alone?" Emma asked.

"Yes." John Taylor swiped at his glasses. "We're stretched thin, with all the extra people upstairs. I'm recruiting some of the other workers."

Emma stepped toward John Taylor. "I am really sorry about Kyle," she said, though her mind was on the unguarded rear lab wall.

"So am I." He cleared his throat again. "He was my best man."

"I know it's hard, but I need you to handle this, John Taylor."

He nodded. "I got it."

"I'll take the wall until you can get a team together to take over." She swallowed hard. "Whoever killed Kyle is still down here. I have to find him before he finds anyone else." A chill ran through her body. "Mason stay and help him."

Emma swung the rifle into her hands, ready to aim and fire, and headed for the wall, moving quickly and silently.

An explosion nearly rocked her off her feet.

CHAPTER TWELVE

Tuesday, December 17th
2207 (10:07 PM)

"Emma?" Mason shouted to her. "Emma, where are you?"

Because he sounded terrified, she didn't give in to exasperation. By now, whoever set that explosion had to know they were close. She started toward the sound of his voice and footfalls and met up with him running full out toward her. "Stop, Mason. Stop."

He slid to a halt, the look in his eyes wild. "Are you okay?"

"I'm fine." He really was terrified. That softened her upset with him.

"What was that?"

"I suspect their backup team has arrived," she said. "You better go check the lab."

"David's got it," he insisted. "You can't walk into whatever you're walking into alone."

There was no sense arguing with him. She knew that look just as he knew her looks. "Have you learned to shoot?"

"Not yet."

"Then stay behind me and stick close—and no unnecessary talking."

He nodded.

At a vee in the tunnel, dust flew, and the wind whipped it
into a choking hazard. She paused and pulled her neck scarf
up over her face, motioning for Mason to do the same.

Walking was difficult. The force of the wind pushed them
back, tugged at their clothes, their eyelids. She shielded as
best she could. Still, every step was a struggle, and that was a
bad sign for what lay ahead.

When they reached what should be the rear wall of the
lab, they stopped. Directly across from it, leading outside,
there was an opening. The mountain had been blown away. A
gaping hole at least twelve feet in diameter let snow and wind
rush into the chamber and right through Emma, chilling her
to the bone.

"The lab's been breached," Mason said, sounding
horrified.

"Stop. Don't go closer," Emma said. "At least one charge is
still active."

"Did you hear me?" he asked her. "The lab wall—the HC
lab's been breached."

"I heard you, Mason."

Mason whipped out his radio and tried to contact David.

Emma waited a long moment. "Well?"

"No response."

He looked torn, warring with himself. "I've got to get to
the lab," he said. "Don't go closer until you hear from me."

She nodded because there was no way he would leave her
otherwise. "Armor up before going in. Full protective gear."

"Right." He started back, then stopped. "Emma, swear
you'll stay put until I radio you."

"Would you go?" She avoided answering him. "The kids are in there. Sophia and David."

Mason turned and ran back down the tunnel, moving much faster running with the brisk wind rather than against it.

Emma watched him until he turned at the vee and disappeared from sight, knowing that might be the last time she ever saw him. Or anyone.

CHAPTER THIRTEEN

MASON ENTERED the lab and stopped short to keep from running into Sophia and the kids. "What are you doing, Sophia?"

She, Olivia and Jacob were dressed in coats and boots. Panic etched her face. "David won't come. I don't want to leave him, but I have to get the children out of here."

Mason stepped between her and the outer door, blocking her path. "No. You can't leave."

Her mouth rounded in an O and she stopped fighting the ties on Jacob's hat at his chin. "But the lab—it's contaminated in there, Mason."

"I know." Mason acknowledged the truth, meeting and holding her gaze, then lowered his voice. "If you've been exposed and you go out there, you'll spread it to others. You need to stay put until we know exactly what we're dealing with here."

Confusion riddled Sophia's face. Torn, she bit down on her lip and her eyes darted back and forth. "But—"

"I know, Sophia." Inside, Mason was crushed at having to tell her this. Outwardly, he held it together, certain she already knew exactly what he meant, but she was in denial. She needed time. Unfortunately, they had little of it. "You and the kids need to shower and scrub, then put on protective gear. Gloves, glasses and masks. I'll grab them for you."

He locked the outer lab door in case the temptation to flee won the battle with logic, retrieved the gear and then passed her the three sets. "Be sure to wash your hair and then cover it with the scrub cap. Tug it down," he motioned with his hand, "to cover the openings in your ears."

The reality of his words sank in deep and Sophia's face tensed even more. If they had been exposed, the damage was already done. Her eyes shone overly bright. "I understand, Dr. M."

"Good. Now, get the children into their quarters and get busy. Put everything all of you are wearing into a bio-hazard bag and set it out in the hallway. I'll take care of it from there." He glanced at the children and then back at Sophia. "This is very important. None of you must come out here again until either David or I come and get you."

She nodded.

"Where is David?" His office sat empty.

"In the inner ring." Sophia's voice shook, and she blinked hard and fast.

"Don't worry. He's suited up, so he's protected," Mason reminded her. "You take the children and go on now. Do all I said. The sooner any spores are off of you, the less likely they are to cause a problem." He smiled for Olivia and Jacob. "Your dad and I will get this mess cleaned up."

"Uncle M., are we going to die?" Olivia stepped closer to him.

"Someday, yes. We all are, Olivia," he said in his best matter-of-fact tone. No way did he dare to lie to her. She'd know it and call him on it in a heartbeat. It would be humiliating to be called out by a nine-year-old girl. Worse, he'd break Olivia's trust. That, he would never willingly do. "But hopefully, that won't be for a long, long time." He nodded for them to go. "Hurry now. Use lots of soap, even on your hair. Don't miss a single spot."

Jacob jutted out his jaw. "I am not putting Bandit in a bio bag, Dr. M."

Dr. M, not Uncle M. Jacob meant business. Mason debated. "Then I'm trusting you to give him the best bath he's ever gotten. It's not a game, Jacob. This is serious. Do you understand?" Mason hoped he didn't come to regret that decision.

Jacob nodded. "So we don't get any germs from him."

"That's right." Mason squatted down to talk eye-to-eye with Jacob. "Can I trust you to do that?"

He nodded. "He'll shower with me. I'll scrub him 'til he's spotless. I promise."

"Thank you, Jacob." Mason straightened.

Sophia pulled the kids to her and they made their way down the hallway to their quarters. When the door shut behind them, Mason swallowed the knot lodged in his throat and walked back toward the outer door where he could see inside the HC lab.

David turned and spotted Mason, standing outside the inner ring. Armored up in protective gear, he stepped over to the glass separating them. His face-shield reflected the overhead lights. David pressed the intercom button. "Stay there, Dr. M." Hand signaling Mason to stay put, David headed for the decontamination chamber.

A few minutes later, he joined Mason in the outer ring. "We've got a problem.""

"I can see that." Shards of rock littered the inner-ring floor. "Seals are definitely breached."

"It's worse than that." Worry and no small measure of fear dragged lines into David's face, alongside his mouth. "The glass is cracked on the Plague case. BP7PP, specifically."

The hair on Mason's neck stood on end. "How bad is it?"

The look in David's eyes went flat. "The container is compromised, and the vial seal is broken." His voice shook. "It's loose in there, Dr. M." He swallowed hard, cast a worried look around. "Where's my family? Did they get out?"

"They can't leave, David." He knew this of course, but his emotions were clouding his judgment. He wanted his family safe. They both did. "They're in isolation in their quarters. Cleaning up, just in case there's been seepage into the outer ring."

David paused to absorb that, then asked, "Did you give Sophia specific instructions?"

"I did, and I gave them all protective gear and instructed them on that, too. I couldn't demand Jacob dispose of Bandit. I realize it's a risk, but I thought it worth taking. Jacob stood up for himself, without any input from Olivia. That's a first." They had all been working toward that for a long time, and the significance of it wasn't lost on David, just as it hadn't been lost on Mason. "He promised to give Bandit a thorough scrubbing." Mason gave David the details to help give him time to adjust to this news.

He tried, but it was hard. The struggle played out across his face and his mouth settled into a flat, straight line. "It's one thing for me to be at risk, but Sophia and the kids..." He looked at Mason with haunted eyes. "I thought I was doing the right thing, bringing them here. Keeping them safe from the storm."

"I know." Mason could only imagine the turmoil going on inside David, but there was no way to soften the blow. David had seen what these pathogens could do. They both had. Mason's stomach flipped. "I thought so, too, or I wouldn't have authorized it." They both shouldered the blame. He only hoped they wouldn't also shoulder the guilt.

David rubbed at his forehead. His hand shook and his voice staggered. "That's not the worst of it."

Could the news get any worse? A deadly pathogen loose in the HC lab. Mason braced. "Tell me. What do you mean?"

"Olivia and Jacob were playing ball. It got away from her and she went after it."

"Olivia's been in the HC lab?" Mason's worry spiked through the ceiling.

"The seal on the vault door is broken. Minor leak, but the decontamination chamber wasn't active, and she was right next to the door when the explosion hit."

Mason needed to lock that down. Take air samples. His mind rushed into overdrive, but he tried to sound calm. "You go check her out," he told David. "I'll let Emma know and do what can be done here."

"I sealed the broken valve and vial as best I could. Then the freezer. Fortunately, only a small section was affected by the blast. The rest held together. Followed protocol and it's all done in there, so stay out," David said. "The vault door seal is the significant thing, and the air. I've already adjusted the air controls inside. It's purifying as fast as possible."

"Good. Good job, David. I'll work on the vault seal. You go reassure your family things are under control. Well, as best you can, considering. And check Olivia thoroughly."

"Dr. M." David cleared his throat, his eyes darted, extra glossy and watery. "She had a broken blister on her hand. All the practicing for basketball."

"She blistered her hand dribbling?"

"No. She burned it making Jacob chocolate chip cookies and then busted the blister dribbling."

His muscles clenched and his breath hitched. "It's open, then?" That mortified Mason. David had to be losing his mind with worry.

"Yeah."

"Take the kit with you and do everything humanly possible to sanitize it and kill the germs."

David turned and hit the hallway in a near run.

An open wound put Olivia deep into the danger zone. Worried sick, Mason radioed Emma. "Come in, E."

A moment later, she answered. "I'm here," she said. "Is everything okay there?"

"No. I'm afraid, it's not." He went on to explain the breach and then the news about Olivia.

"Is she going to be okay?"

"It's too soon to know." He let her hear his concern. "Pray for her."

"I will." Emma said and meant it; no misunderstanding that tone. "Mason, have you been exposed?"

He hesitated, then finally answered. "Maybe. I'm not sure yet."

"I'll be there in ten."

"No!" His response was swift and stern. "No, Emma. You can't come in. Not until I've done all I can do and the outer ring tests safe."

Her radio went silent.

"Did you hear me, Emma?" When she didn't answer, he deepened his tone. "Don't you play that you're-not-hearing-me card because you don't want to hear me, and don't even think about coming back here before I give you an all-clear, Emma."

"But I could help you."

She could. But he didn't want her help. He wanted her safe. "This is my wheelhouse and I don't need help right now. Don't get all offended. All I mean is it's bad enough David and his family are here." He paused, but she didn't say anything, so he added, "We know of one. What if there are more invaders? Who will be left to take care of them and keep this stuff from spreading?"

"Okay, fine." Emma sniffed. "But, Mason, don't you dare die on me. I will be so ticked off at you, I'll go into hell itself to bless you out for getting yourself killed. You hear me?"

His heart leapt in his chest. She was worried and emotional about him. Really worried and emotional. Emma rarely let anyone see her emotional or vulnerable. She genuinely cared about him. Threatening to march into hell to blister his ears? That was as open and real and genuine as Emma Miller had ever been in her life. "I will do my best not to inconvenience you, Emma."

"That would be greatly appreciated."

Mason bit his elation from his lips. They insisted on curving into a smile, and at the moment, that just wasn't appropriate. No matter how long awaited, inappropriate. "David sealed the lab wall. Not sure it'll be totally effective, but so far, testing shows it's holding."

"That's a good sign."

"How are things on that end?"

"Busy."

He quizzed her about what she'd done to assure proper protocols were in place. From her descriptions, they were. At this point, that didn't surprise him. Emma was a resourceful, knowledgeable woman with abilities that far exceeded his expectations. "You safe there?"

"I'm surrounded by a crew John Taylor pulled off construction. A dozen men, all armed and standing watch."

"John Taylor had that many guns in Security?"

"I didn't ask where they got the weapons." She hedged. "They do have them, but they have limited ammo. They also have a variety of tools, which can be formidable weapons, should the need arise."

A stray thought occurred to Mason and it worried him enough that he put a question to Emma. "Are you sure none of them are part of the backup team?"

"John Taylor vouched for every one of them—and they're wearing neon armbands, so I know they're on our side and don't shoot them."

Mason almost smiled. John Taylor certainly respected her skills. "Good thinking."

"He's impressively competent, Mason. I fear he's often underestimated, but only by fools."

"He is, and you're right not to minimize the value of the crew's tools. A nail gun can be wickedly effective."

"Indeed, it can."

"I've got to get busy here," he said, reluctant to break contact with her. "Keep me posted, and do not come to the lab, Emma. I mean it. Don't make me change the code and lock you out."

"That's not necessary. I promise, I won't," she said. "But only because that would cause you more worry."

He forgot shielding his heart and games and banter and answered honestly. "It would. I want you safe."

She was equally honest. "I want you safe, too."

He stilled, mentally staggering. After all these years, it was hard to believe. But maybe all those years ago her mother had been right...

CHAPTER FOURTEEN

HAVING REPORTED the breach to Liz earlier, Emma called her again now to fill her in on the details and give her the latest update on consequences. In the mouth of the tunnel near the lab's rear wall, she leaned back and accepted the truth. If she had a job after this mission, it'd be a miracle. "Yes, I can talk now," Emma said, the frigid air fogging her breath.

"Human costs?"

"One fatality and one possible direct exposure." Her emotions in riot, Emma tamped them down. "Close proximity to the blast on the exposure."

"And the fatality?"

"Gunshot. Twice to the back of the head."

"Them or us?"

Liz was asking who had done the shooting. "Them."

"Who was the victim?"

"Kyle Greer. Security staff member." John Taylor was

91

really upset about Kyle's death. Who wouldn't be? Seeing someone who works for you lying shot to death on their way to taking a position you ordered them to take... of course, it was upsetting. Not John Taylor's fault, but certainly upsetting. Emma hadn't prevented the death. That was upsetting to her, too. "Greer was assigned to guard the lab's rear wall. It appears he was on his way to it." The position his body was in indicated that clearly. "Looks like he was ambushed from behind." Blessing or curse, Kyle had never seen it coming.

"Is his post covered now?" Liz asked, her voice amazingly calm and neutral.

"It is, yes." Emma scanned the tunnel and the opening to the outside near the rear lab wall. All seemed well. "Security Chief, John Taylor Moore, recruited a crew of construction workers to assist. A dozen men. They've been issued masks and gloves. Had their own eye protection."

"No suits?"

"Not enough available. But they've been briefed and are aware their clothing has to be disposed of before leaving the area, and how to do so properly."

"With the storm parked over you, that's about the best you can do, Emma."

In the distance, the wind howled in the tunnels. At her point in the tunnel, there was a chilly breeze. "It is."

"These construction workers know the risks, right?"

"They do," Emma said. "I disclosed only what I had to for the importance of the instructions to be understood. They were told the truth about how this could impact their health, possibly kill them."

"And they stepped up anyway." Liz let out a sigh. "Amazing courage."

It was amazing. "They're parents and sons and spouses and they want their families safe. And they want others' families safe." They were incredible people. Exceptional. Admirable.

"So, what about the possible exposure? You said the person's blast proximity was a factor."

"Yes, it was." Olivia's image filled Emma's mind. She blinked hard and focused. "It's David's daughter, Olivia, Liz. She was near the vault door when the blast occurred. Seal was broken on the vault door in the blast. Olivia has an open burn blister on her hand. I know with Holly getting antibiotics here is impossible, but we need them...just in case someone contracts." Emma stepped out far enough to scan the men John Taylor had positioned all throughout the chamber. The temperature dropped due to the jagged hole to the outside, leaving no doubt how the backup team had entered the area. All of the men on the crew looked alert and watchful. And resigned. "She's confined to quarters in quarantine at the moment with her mother and brother."

"Were they exposed, too?"

Emma stepped back into the tunnel. "They were with her after she was exposed, so indirectly, yes."

"I hate this." Liz let out a puff of breath. "What exactly would they be contracting? Do we know?"

Emma hated it, too. Thoroughly and completely. "Black plague." She dropped her voice even lower. "Weaponized."

"No." Liz gasped. "Why didn't they tell us that before?"

"They haven't told us now. I realized it when pulling the lab inspection. I asked, and Mason confirmed it."

"The director is going to have a stroke," Liz predicted. "Emma, we wouldn't have put you in the position had we known."

"You wouldn't have wanted to put me in this position, but you would have done it, Liz. You wouldn't have a choice because I am here and protecting this lab is more important than any one life."

"Weaponized Black Plague," Liz said, as if scanning her memory. "Is there an antidote for that?"

Emma's stomach fluttered and sank. "No."

"Nothing?"

"Nothing." Emma's stomach sank a little lower. Mason had told her that much. Deeming it best not to dwell on that, she moved on. "Do you have an ID on any of the invaders?"

"Not yet. The team at headquarters is working on it."

Disappointed with that news, Emma squeezed her eyes shut. Flying blind was something she always tried to avoid. "Sooner we get that information, the better."

"Insights would help. I know. They are trying."

"I'm sure they are," Emma said. They didn't want a nightmare on their hands any more than the people guarding the chamber or in the lab wanted to die. "It's just been a lot of drama. This little Olivia..." Emma felt emotion welling and let it. "She's something else, Liz."

"I can hear that she is in your voice." Liz shifted subjects, as if sensing they both needed a brief mental break to ratchet down the tension and emotional strain. "Not that we have to talk about it now, but I'm curious about something."

Grateful for the reprieve, Emma sniffed. "What?"

"Was Dr. Hunk forty pounds overweight and married with kids?"

Emma chuckled under her breath. "Actually, he's single, more muscular than he was and, unfortunately, still very much a hunk."

"I might faint. I'm definitely envious." Lisa let out an exaggerated sigh. "What's wrong with you? You actually sound disappointed."

Emma stared at the edge of the rock wall near the mouth of the tunnel that opened to the outside. Beyond the hole, wind whipped the snow and a concrete barricade stretched out of her line of sight. On the far side of the barricade was a crane. On it, a wrecking ball hung suspended from chain. Cables stretched over the machine to hold it tied down and in place. Why hadn't they lowered the wrecking ball? It wasn't moving, so it had to be tied down, but it should have been lowered to the ground and secured. "Honestly, I am disappointed."

"Why?" Liz sounded totally baffled. "Is he still giving you the cold shoulder?"

"More like the deep freeze." She hoped her disappointment about that didn't come through in her voice. "He's cooperative and even a little concerned about me. But mostly, he's a lot confused, and still distant about anything personal." Maybe a little angry, too, though she couldn't imagine why he would be, so she didn't mention it to Liz.

"Well, you are posing as a reporter who's been given authority over him and his lab. That's bound to have his hackles up at least a little. He knows you, Emma, and he knows you aren't being straight with him. Considering it all, his is a pretty normal response, don't you think?"

Emma hated to admit it was, but personal integrity required it. She swept at the dust beneath her feet with the toe of her shoe. "Yeah, I do."

"Yet you still resent the deep freeze."

"Well, yeah." Emma paced a short path down the tunnel and back again. "I mean, he does know me, but he really doesn't. Or he doesn't think much of me. If he did, he'd give me some credit for being a decent human being."

"If he's a little concerned instead of a lot concerned, isn't that some credit?"

"I guess, but mostly I'm getting the deep freeze, Liz." Emma was confusing herself with all these conflicting emotions and feelings about him. "You know what? Let's just forget it. It's not important."

"Let's don't."

Emma stilled. "Why not?"

"Because I think it's very important," Liz said. "You don't typically care what others think about you or what you're doing. But you care a lot about what he thinks."

Did she? The truth seeped inside. Well, she guessed she did. No. That was a coward's response. The truth was, she did care. She always had. Admitting it was hard and left her a little bewildered. How had he gotten that kind of power over her? Clueless, she grunted. "Silly, isn't it?"

"I don't think it is silly, Emma. I think you care because he matters to you. Maybe in ways none of the others did. Maybe he always has mattered, and maybe he always will."

Liz's words resonated so deep they had Emma shaking down to the soles of her feet. She stiffened and walked quickly back to the tunnel's mouth and then looked out, checking the guys near the rear wall, then those near the hole to the outside. Mason had rejected her most of her life. Guarding against that kind of hurt happening again, she willed her protective shields to slide up and lock into place. "I don't know if I'd go that far."

"I would," Liz countered. "Remember all the broken engagements and potential relationships that haven't worked out?"

Emma's face burned. "You know, Liz, I'm starting to regret ever telling you any of that."

"Don't bother. I'm not judging you."

"What are you doing then?"

"Merely pointing out that when you talk about the doc, you get this tone in your voice. It's special. Through all the others, one date, a couple weeks or months, or even engaged, I've never heard that tone in your voice when you talked about any of them. Never, Emma. Think about that."

"I don't want to think about it." She smacked her heel

down hard in the dust. "I want to get beyond it and never think about it again."

"Why? Are you seriously eager for more of the same?" Liz grunted. "No. Go the distance, Em. That's my best advice. You know what they say about a deep freeze."

She had no idea. "What do they say?"

"It never lasts forever. Sometimes you have to hang tight until it thaws out."

The temptation to make an attempt was great, but common sense prevailed. "Not happening, Liz." Emma scuffed the toe of her shoe and drew a circle. "This is not the right time or place or circumstance. Who needs the distraction?" It'd be futile anyway. Emma could hang tight for a lifetime and Mason would still resist and reject her. *Buffet.*

"Just keep an open mind, okay? You never know." Something on Liz's end buzzed in the background. "Oh, man."

"What?"

"Dr. Hunk is calling me."

Emma frowned. "That's bad news?"

"The worst. If it wasn't, headquarters would be calling."

Emma wasn't tracking Liz's line of thought. The HC lab was breached, they had a fatality and potential exposure. "The situation here is critical, Liz."

"Critical just escalated. Him calling me direct means one thing."

"What?"

"The entire lab has been breached."

"Oh, no." Mason. Mason had been exposed? He hadn't told her. Why hadn't he told her? "Call me back as soon as you can." Emma ended the call in a cold sweat, her nerves punching through her skin as if they were attached on the outside.

But it wasn't Liz who called Emma back. It was Mason, and he confirmed the horrible news. "The lab was compromised. It's now secure, and air samples are testing okay and improving. Fortunately, David made essential adjustments to the purification system right away."

That didn't sound so bad. "And...?"

"Olivia's been exposed through the open wound."

"Yes, you told me that," Emma said, confused about what had changed. "A ruptured blister on her hand."

He hesitated and his tone tensed. "After testing her, David feels it's highly probable she'll contract."

"Oh, no." Every muscle seemed to lockdown at once. Emma stiffened against them. Her stomach curdled. She swallowed a lump in her throat. "If Olivia contracts, how long will it be before she becomes symptomatic?"

"Best estimate, a few hours." Mason paused. "Remember, Emma. These pathogens are...special. Data isn't readily shared. That said, I can't see it taking longer than that and being effective."

Chills coursed through Emma, head to toe. "Then you better get on the phone with headquarters and find someone in that little need-to-know loop fast."

"I have. The request is working its way up the chain."

What more could he do? "What do you know?"

"If she's been infected," Mason said, "then she needs antibiotics right away."

Emma assessed his disclosure. "You want to treat her preemptively."

"I can't, Emma," he said, his voice curt. "If I could, don't you think I would?"

He was upset and disturbed. Naturally. He was close to Olivia and the whole family. Emma blew off his sharp retort and asked, "Okay, you can't. But why not?"

"We don't have antibiotics on the premises. They work on the base form of this, but this isn't that. Antibiotic therapy is an arrow in the wind, but at the moment, it's the only arrow we've got in our quiver." He didn't sound at all happy about that. Actually, he resented it deeply. "With Holly raging like a maniac outside, no one can get anything to us, and we can't get out to get anything."

They had no antibiotics and no defense weaponry, and at least one invading murderer on the loose inside the facility. Emma rubbed a knot from the muscle in her neck, scanned the tunnel she'd been exploring when he'd called. "Liz is working on this, too—trying to get supplies to us." He needed to know she had already asked.

"She told me," he said, disclosing they'd spoken. "She is trying, but odds aren't in our favor. Not with winds nearly a hundred miles per hour blowing snow and ice. Everything is shut down tighter than a drum out there."

"I'll call her again and update her on the potential severity. I don't know what else we can do." Liz might come up with an unorthodox idea. She often did. "If Olivia shows symptoms, then how long does she have before…" Emma couldn't say it. She could barely think the word die, much less when it related to the precious little girl.

"Once she's symptomatic, my best guess is less than eight hours. Maybe sooner." The pain that revelation brought Mason reflected in his voice. "She'll steadily decline and then…die."

CHAPTER FIFTEEN

TUESDAY, December 18th
0330 (3:30 AM)

LIZ DIDN'T ANSWER her phone, so Emma left a message for her to call as soon as she could and then returned to inspecting the tunnels. If the team of invaders had come down through one of the entrances that led to the offices on the first sub-street level rather than entering the tunnels through the biometric elevator, they could have just walked down to the opening that left the lab's rear wall vulnerable.

She'd searched all the tunnels now but had found no hard evidence of the initial team's ingress or egress. John Taylor had restricted access to all tunnels, limiting it to his staff and the construction crew standing guard at the lab's rear wall. All other employees on the premises had been reassigned from their regular duties to helping care for the five-thousand stranded passengers and to prevent any of them from entering the tunnels.

Emma had seen no signs of foot traffic or abandoned

carts, or trucks. No drag marks in the dust or new scuffs on the tunnel walls. No overhead lights not lit up, and no people. While the backup team's entry was evident by the hole in the mountain to the outside, the initial team's entry point remained a mystery. Nothing had been found that could be remotely identified as the path they'd taken to enter the tunnels.

She checked her watch. They'd had five hours without another incident and, while she was grateful for that, she'd seen the tactic used before. *Lull your enemy into complacency. Then attack.* In this situation, that's exactly what she'd do. Wait until the guards got comfortable, then bored and sleepy. That was the backup team's best odds for success—and she'd warned the men against that. Hopefully, they had taken the warning to heart. Considering their necks were on the line, she felt certain they had.

The phone clipped to her waist vibrated, signaling an incoming call. *Liz.* Emma snagged it. "Miller."

"Emma, sorry. Been tied up with headquarters, trying to get clearances resolved so we can learn more about what we're facing."

"I understand," Emma said. She stopped and leaned back against a tunnel wall, propping her foot behind her. "Liz, I need a miracle."

"Above my pay-grade," she said. "But I'll do what I can."

Emma already knew the response but called for the supplies again anyway. "I need the best antibiotic and treatment for exposure to BP7PP, and I need weapons and ammo. I have one rifle, and I'm low on ammo. That's it. I know Greer's killer is down here somewhere. No sign of him or the backup team yet. I'm nearly done inspecting the most likely tunnels. Unless they dropped in via skyhook, I'm bound to encounter direct conflict shortly."

"Situation understood," Liz said. "And I know Olivia has a

high probability of being infected. I'm doing everything I can, and that's the truth."

A lump in Emma's throat settled. She absently rubbed her upper chest. Her clothes were gritty from the dust. "Are you getting anywhere with headquarters?"

"They've been briefed on all developments. Now, they're walking through the request, but they've already warned me that there is no antidote."

"I know that. We all know that." Emma shut her eyes and demanded the bite leave her tone. Time was too scarce to rehash old ground. If Olivia contracted, she would die. "If they release all the clinical records and research to Mason, maybe he can come up with something."

"That's the argument we've both been making. Headquarters counters with if it were that easy, they'd have done it long ago. It's not. Mason fought the good fight on the conference call with head honcho, so we'll see how it works out. He earned my respect, I'll tell you that. We should know something before long."

Mason had always had more guts than sense, and if he was determined, nothing swayed him. She'd loved that resolve in him. Now it fed on the sense of urgency gripping Emma hard. "Olivia likely doesn't have any time to waste."

"I know. Mason told me she's at high risk to contract." Liz did know, and she too was feeling the strain of possibly losing a child. "But for now, we've done all we can do."

Emma wanted to scream until someone did more than think. Until they acted. She bit her bitterness back and forced a calm she didn't feel into her voice. "Right."

"I do have identities on two of the invaders from your photos. Both are foreign nationals. Wealthy, well educated—in Australia—and members of CAR."

"Central Asian Resistance?" Based on looks, they didn't fit the profile. "The Stans?"

"Yes," Liz said. "Tajikistan, I'm told, but it could be any of them. Kazakhstan, Kyrgyzstan, Tajikistan, Turkmenistan, Afghanistan or Uzbekistan. The waters get a little muddy on intel coming out of there."

The waters were always muddy on intel coming out of there. Nomadic people and the Silk Road made for a crossroads for the movement of people, goods and technology. Ideas, too, especially with Europe and Western, South and East Asia.

"These two, like many, have strong Russian ties, but also Ukrainian."

"Ukrainian?" Emma stared off into space. "Why do they want BP7PP?"

"Leverage. Same as everyone else," Liz said, sounding resigned.

"Tell me what you know about them from a tactical perspective."

"CAR favors five-man teams. Your one murderer on the loose most likely makes your fifth person. Two or more team-members could be females."

"Got it." Emma lowered her propped foot to the ground. "Anything else notable?"

"Not that you don't already know."

Emma's first mission had been in that area of the world. She'd been prepped and tested. Nothing like a trial by fire to burn details into your memory. "I'll send more video as soon as the line's free." She started heading back to the rear of the lab, where the construction crew stood sentry. "The invaders blasted through the rock and they would now have entry access directly into the lab if not for the makeshift wall we've put into place, Liz." No doubt, Liz would be as unhappy as Emma with that.

"Access to the HC lab proper, or the outer ring?"

"Proper," Emma said. "The outer ring doesn't encircle the entire HC lab's inner ring."

"Naturally." Liz's sigh crackled in Emma's ear. "It's the lab's rear wall that isn't encircled, right?"

"Right," Emma said. "That solves the mystery of why they blasted through at all."

"I guess I missed a step. I'm not tracking you."

"Blowing out the rear wall of the inner lab was the shortest, the most vulnerable and the most direct route into the HC lab's inner hub." Emma stared up at nothing at all. "If so few know this place exists, then I'm wondering how the invaders knew about it?"

"An insider?" Liz suggested.

"How else could they know?" Emma twisted her mouth. "You need to look into that."

"I will. And I'll talk to headquarters. I trust my sources there. They'll dig deep."

"Follow the money first." Emma grimaced. "It's always about money with CAR."

"Will do."

Standing up ahead, John Taylor spotted Emma's approach and headed toward her. "Sounds good, Liz. I've got to go," Emma said, and ended the call.

Shifting her attention to the Security Chief, she asked, "Any news, John?" Maybe everyone else around here consistently called him John Taylor, but if he didn't object, she'd appreciate shortening it.

"John Taylor," he said, correcting her. "John was my father. He was not a good man."

Guess that was a bad idea. "I'm sorry, John Taylor. Any news?"

Dirt-smudged and weary, he still looked even more tense than Emma felt. "Four men were spotted violating the lock-down and leaving the terminal," he said. "Security cameras picked them up outside Terminal C. I thought you'd want a look at them." He manipulated his phone, then passed it to her.

On the footage, four men dressed like the ones neutralized in black tactical gear were moving away from the terminal and getting into a waiting black van. With all the heavy equipment around here, she couldn't get five miles to a drugstore, but they could get out in a van? That made zero sense. "Any of the cameras pick up a tag?"

"Not on that footage, but another camera got it." He wiggled his fingers, signaling her to pass the phone. She did, and he took it, maneuvered to the right footage, and then passed the phone back to her. "It's on that one."

She watched the short video, and her heart dropped into her stomach. "Diplomatic tags? Seriously?"

"Seriously." John Taylor's expression sobered even more. "They're leaving the airport on the next video. Which tells me they're determined but short on sense or they wouldn't risk the storm. We'll likely find them in a snowbank or a ditch somewhere close." He rubbed at his chin. "Them leaving also says they got what they wanted here."

Emma feared he was right, yet, aside from leaving the airport, the evidence didn't support that conclusion. "If they wanted to get the pathogen, they failed."

John Taylor squinted. "But if they wanted to infect the five-thousand people in the terminal, set a pandemic into motion, then maybe they didn't fail." He gave Emma a bold, steady look that chilled her to the bone. "Dr. M. says the one they were after is highly contagious. Doesn't take long to spread."

He had a point. It wasn't consistent with CAR's normal operations. They were after the money. They would want the virus to black-market sell it. To use it as leverage against other entities or governments. But if they wanted to breach a vial and contaminate the facility and those in it, then they had accomplished their mission. At least, they would leave confident they had succeeded. Fortunately, David and Mason had been onsite and immediately available to take steps to prevent a widespread contamination. If the lab hadn't been shut down for the move, containment would have been far more complex. They might not have had complete success. They might not, anyway. Olivia ran through Emma's mind. "It'd be anomalous, but it's possible," Emma said to John Taylor. "Where's your emergency medical officer?"

"Snowed in at home." John Taylor frowned. "He tried for hours to get here but couldn't."

"Can you take me to his office?" she asked. "I need some medical supplies."

"If you're after antibiotics for Olivia, Emma, I can save you the trip." Regret burned in John Taylor's eyes. "There aren't any."

More bad news. Catching a break, just once, would be great. "You've personally looked?"

"I have." John Taylor nodded, lending weight to his claim. "Came up dry. I called the medical officer to verify. He said they don't keep any pharmaceuticals onsite except aspirin."

Emma bit back her disappointment. "When someone needs something, where do they get it?"

"Portal Drugs. It delivers."

Hope soared. "How far is the store from here?"

"About three miles off campus, so about five miles total. But it might as well be a thousand miles. You aren't getting five miles in that storm, Emma. If it were possible, I'd have gone myself."

"All the heavy equipment around here, and we have nothing that will get us five miles?"

"Not in a hundred mile-per-hour winds." He lifted his hands. "It's suicide."

There had to be a way. She had to keep thinking.

"I hate it, too, but it's a dead-end, Emma. Forget it. Focus on what you can do," he said, then suddenly stilled and his eyes took on a faraway look, signaling some thought had hit him and he was weighing it.

"What?" She prodded him. He definitely had something in mind. It was written all over his face. "Will you answer me?"

"It was just an idea. Won't work. Sorry." He hitched his pants. "You should get to the lab." Compassion burned in John Taylor's eyes. "Mason could use some help from someone who is thinking straight and is not terrified of losing his daughter."

"Will he let me in?" He'd been adamant she not return earlier.

"He's got the outer ring decontaminated." John Taylor nodded. "Don't worry. I've got this down here. Anything at all odd happens, I'll call you right away."

"Thanks, John Taylor." Emma took off back down the tunnel toward the lab, eager to see Mason with her own eyes. To know he was okay.

CHAPTER SIXTEEN

Tuesday, December 18th
0413 (4:13 AM)

GLAD MASON HADN'T FOLLOWED through on his threat and changed the code, Emma left the tunnel and entered the lab through the outer door.

Changes had occurred in the outer ring. A row of four security monitors had been set up on a long table positioned near the coat hooks. She checked the screens, recognized the views of Terminals A, B and C and the tented area called the Main. A fifth monitor sat on a desk beside the table holding the four. On the screen was a live shot of David's family's quarters. Olivia was stretched out in bed, the covers pulled up to her chin. Her shower cap was slightly askew. Her mother adjusted it from her seat beside Olivia's bed. Sophia looked calm, but she had to be scared half out of her mind. Jacob had a stranglehold on Bandit. He stood against the wall, away from Olivia but close enough that he could talk to her. Sophia kept talking to her children, reassuring them they would all be fine. How did she manage to sound so convincing using hushed tones? Emma's mother would have been hysterical.

Sophia looked at the camera and her mask slipped. The fear etching into her face nearly knocked Emma to her knees. One thing was clear. Sophia was a strong woman. Strong and determined to not give up hope. Not to let her children be afraid. Not to lose her daughter without a fight.

Emma admired that, and wondered if in that position, how she would react. She honestly couldn't imagine. Getting too emotional, Emma backed away and looked around. Where was Mason? David? Both of their offices were empty.

She would solve that puzzle in a minute. First, she had to talk to Liz. She retrieved her phone from its case at her waist, then called.

"Hi, Emma."

"Liz, I have a priority update."

"Go ahead." She paused, then added, "Recording now."

"Four unidentified men violated lockdown and left the terminal via a black van with diplomatic tags." Emma continued, reeling off the tag number and descriptions of each of the men. "A fifth man was driving."

"Not one of the original backup team-members?"

"No. An additional man." Emma scratched her cheek. "John Taylor believes he was in the facility beforehand. He's matched him to a man blending in as a passenger. We have several frames of him in security footage before the escape. The frames and footage of their departure is in your inbox. So are photos."

"I'll get an APB issued on that right away. With the storm, they won't get far."

"I've warned the Chief that they could double back here so to stay on alert."

"Good. They'd have to be desperate to return after a clean

exit. My main concern is it'll be tricky to stop and detain them with diplomatic immunity."

Emma had a plan. "Tell them they were exposed to a lethal pathogen, and if they don't want to die to do what authorities say."

"That'd work for me. Might not go over too well with law enforcement, though. They'll understand by intercepting these men, they're exposing themselves to the pathogen as well."

"It will go over fine if you bring them into the loop." Emma pointed out.

"So, the four—and their driver—haven't been exposed?"

"As far as we can tell with certainty, only the inner ring was contaminated," Emma said, being deliberately cagey. "However, there are cracks in the lab's rear wall. They've been repaired. If those repairs have been a hundred percent effective, then no, they haven't been exposed. But if they haven't..."

"You're saying we can't determine exposure with certainty at this time."

Testing had come out fine. Air samples had been fine. Neither Mason nor Emma had found any evidence of leakage. Emma stiffened her spine and served the mission. "Odds are against it, but that's what I'm saying."

Liz got it. "I'll bet the construction crew on the rear wall was glad to hear they weren't exposed. You and John Taylor, too."

"I am, and they will be when they know it. We're trying to determine absolute facts before saying anything more." The courageous construction crew volunteered to guard fearing the worst. *Admirable*. She didn't want to tell them they would be fine and then have to tell them they wouldn't. Emma stared at the security screen of Olivia. Her face was still animated. She was talking with Jacob. "The medical officer is stranded off-site and they don't keep meds in the facility. If an occasion arises, they use a drug store about five miles away."

"I see where you're headed with this," Liz cut in. "Emma, you are not going to that store."

"Yes, Liz, I am." Emma put a steel in her voice she'd never heard before herself. "If I don't, in the matter of a few hours, we could have a dead little girl."

"I understand, okay? But you need to think bigger picture right now. You're responsible for that lab. If you leave, who is left to prevent the backup team from circling back and emptying it? You said yourself, they can't get far in this storm. Dr. Hunk can't shoot. John Taylor's too far away," Liz said, then added, "You can't make a five-mile trip and then make it five-miles back in this storm. Bottle your emotions and think. Just logic and reason, Emma. Downed power lines, falling trees, strong winds. You'd be lucky to get beyond the facility grounds."

"I have to try," Emma insisted, elevating her voice. Mason loved Olivia. Her whole family loved her. And Jacob needed her. "If she gets sick, I can't just let her die."

Jacob gasped. He was watching Emma. Was the monitor a two-way? From the devastated expression on his face, the way he clutched Bandit to his face, it was, and he had heard her. Emma's heart sank. "I've got to go." She clipped the phone back to her waist. "Jacob. Can you hear me?"

He nodded and spun away.

"Jacob, wait. Please, wait."

He kept going until he ran straight into Sophia.

Feeling like the lowliest slug, Emma mouthed, "Sorry. I didn't know…"

Sophia nodded, then comforted her son.

Emma walked out of camera view toward the glass wall between the outer and inner rings. "Mason." She spotted him. He and David were inside the HC lab proper. She scanned the HC lab damage. The repairs they had made. The sealant applied over the cracks in the freezer glass-door. There was no doubt about it. The invaders had been after the BP7PP.

Walking closer, Emma reached up to the wall and tapped the intercom system used to talk back-and-forth between the outer ring and the HC inner ring areas of the lab. "Did they get it, Mason?"

"No." He paused and looked at Emma through the glass. "They broke one of the vials, though. Percussion, it appears."

Emma's skin crept. "It's loose in there?"

"Yes, but we've completed the protocols to neutralize and sealed the freezer."

"How can you neutralize if there's no antidote?"

"There's a difference in neutralizing and treating, Emma. We killed it. Can we get into the specifics later?"

"I need to know, Mason," she insisted. "Did Olivia experience direct exposure?" Had she entered the inner ring?

He stopped what he was doing and walked over to the glass wall. "She was close to the vault door, chasing a ball. The force of the blast..."

David interjected. "I was on my way in. She chased the ball in after me." Anguish flooded his face. "Bottom line, she got sprayed with the sample."

Oh, God. Olivia needed those meds desperately. They wouldn't cure her, but maybe they would slow things down and give them time to come up with something to help her. Something to kill it in her. It was a long-shot. Totally irrational, probably. But it was hope. She had to hold on to hope. "My associate is moving heaven and earth, trying to get medicines to us."

He stepped closer still, so she could see his eyes. "I know Emma. Everything that can be done is being done."

Her eyes burned. She blinked hard and fast. "Hurry and get out of there, okay?"

"We're doing our best."

She let him see her fear, her concern for him. "Do better, all right?"

He locked their gazes, and his expression softened. "I'll try my hardest. I promise."

"Okay." She nodded. "Okay."

"Okay." He turned back to what he was doing.

Fighting tears, she shut down the intercom, her hand shaking.

CHAPTER SEVENTEEN

TUESDAY, December 18th
0545 (5:45 AM)

IN THE KITCHEN, Emma wolfed down a piece of buttered toast and a cup of coffee. She was about to raid the refrigerator when her radio blared. "Emma? Emma?"

John Taylor's voice, and he sounded strained and agitated. She swallowed fast. "This is Emma." The bite of toast stuck in her throat. She gulped down hot coffee. "Go ahead."

"I need clout at the Main right now. Janette knows about Greer and she is freaking out. She's seen the body."

Shock pumped through Emma. "All of them?"

"No. Thank heaven. Just Greer. I couldn't put him with the thugs."

Great. Just great. Emma rinsed her cup at the sink. "I'm on my way."

"She doesn't know you. Mason needs to get up to the Main. That's where she is right now."

"He can't." Mason was in running lab tests on Olivia. "I'm on my way."

Abandoning the kitchen, Emma headed down the hallway toward the outer door. When she moved past the monitors, Mason intercepted her. "Emma."

She stopped and turned, saw him standing there. Tense and stiff, as if only by sheer will he was holding himself together. The agony in his expression was too palpable to misunderstand. The tests had been completed. The results were in. "It's positive."

Mason nodded. Beside him, on the screen in the quarantined quarters, Sophia collapsed against David. Jacob and Olivia were asleep. "She's contracted it, Emma." Mason choked up.

"Don't give up. Get creative," Emma said. She hadn't wanted to do what she was about to suggest, but now she had no choice. "There are a lot of people upstairs. "Maybe someone has antibiotics on them."

John Taylor, listening in on his radio, groaned. "Janette will never allow you to canvass the passengers."

"We can't do that." Mason objected. "We'd have to expose the lab."

"No, we wouldn't," Emma said. "And I'm not going to let Olivia get sicker and sicker because Janette will get upset. That is *not* happening."

"If you tell her, she will stop you," John Taylor warned Emma.

"Then I won't tell her."

Mason was more pragmatic. "I'm not going to bother trying to stop you. I've seen that look on you before and won't waste your time or mine. I will say be careful." Mason grimaced. "Going above, you'll be unarmed, Emma."

"Dr. M., she can't—"

"She will, John Taylor," Mason said. "The woman sometimes has more guts than sense, but she's doing what she has to do, and we have to trust her. If Janette does go toe-to-toe with her... well, just trust Emma."

"Yes, sir."

Emma heard the skepticism in John Taylor's voice. It told her more than his words. He feared Janette. "I know it's risky," Emma told them both. "And I will be careful, but I am going to do it."

"Have you cleared this through Liz?" Mason asked.

She'd forbid it. Her concern was the lab. Emma's concern was the lab *and* Olivia. She couldn't lie to him, so she ignored the question.

Thankfully, he understood and didn't ask it again.

Appreciating Mason's backing her and the additional argument reprieve, Emma headed to the outer door, confiscated a cart parked near it, and then raced to the elevator, driving nearly as fast as Mason had the first time he'd driven her down to the lab.

John Taylor stood inside the open elevator. The grated metal door stood slats open and waiting for her. When she stepped inside, John Taylor groused. "Figured you'd need the code."

She had committed it to memory but saw no sense in disclosing that if she didn't have to do it. "Thanks." Emma stepped back, deeper into the elevator.

The door closed and the ride up started. "Don't give Janette any advance warning," John Taylor said. "She says to stop you, and her minions will do whatever it takes to stop you. They know her, and they know their jobs are on the line if they dare to cross her." He shrugged. "I've got your back, but there's only one of me."

And his job would be on the line, too. Especially if Graystone failed to return. "No problem. I've got this," Emma said. The woman would never see her coming.

The elevator stopped and they walked out together and into the Main proper. It was crowded and busy and, considering the early hour, fewer were sleeping than Emma had expected there would be. Briefcase Man, the one she'd noticed multiple times before, fell in behind her.

"Do you know him?" Emma asked John Taylor. Maybe the man was an undercover member of his staff.

"He's been hanging around here for three days. We've been watching him closely, but he hasn't made a move that could even be considered suspicious."

That was before the airport had been closed. Before the storm had unleashed on them. "Three days warrants asking him who he is and why he's here."

"I thought so, too." John Taylor coughed. "But Dr. M. vetoed me."

Mason knew Briefcase Man—or knew about him, then. "He's one of theirs?" That would have been a handy piece of information for someone to have shared with her.

"To be honest, I don't know who he is, but Dr. M. vouched for him." John Taylor glanced her way. "That's good enough for me."

Because John Taylor trusted Mason.

Emma wound through the crowd to the buzz of hushed voices. It was kind of people to be mindful of those sleeping around them. A clump of media, including Darcy Keller, had gathered under a tent in a roped-off area. Janette stood with them. She looked a little stunned, but as if she were trying to harness it. A gaggle of microphones stood set up on a wooden podium. The airport's logo was on its front in big, bold letters.

John Taylor stepped closer to Emma. "I need to back off or she'll sense something is coming and intercede. I'll be close by."

"No problem." Emma veered away from him and toward the microphone.

Janette didn't appear formidable, just all business in her tailored tan suit and heels, her blond hair pulled back from her face in a somewhat severe looking knot at her nape. Engrossed in conversation with a seated Darcy Keller, Janette didn't notice Emma, so Emma ignored the women and went straight to the microphone. "May I have your attention? Attention, please."

Janette swirled toward Emma, strode double-time toward her.

John Taylor stepped in and blocked her. "Don't."

"Who is she?" Janette demanded to know. "Who are you?" she called out to Emma. "I demand an answer immediately."

"Cut those cameras, right now," Emma said, motioning with her hand.

Red lights went off, but one remained. "I said now. Unless you want to be banned from this facility and tossed outside, do it."

The light went out and Emma focused on Janette. "Lower your voice. You'll frighten the passengers."

Janette glared at her, resenting the instruction, and turned to John Taylor. "Where's Dr. Martin?"

"Dr. Martin is currently unavailable," Emma answered.

Sliding her a sidelong look, Janette put a bite in her tone. "Who are you?"

"I'm Dr. Martin's boss." Emma paused for that to sink in, then swiveled her gaze to one of the cameramen. "Is this being broadcast to the other terminals?"

Janette didn't answer.

Darcy Keller did. "It is."

"Thank you," Emma said, then turned back to the mike. Everyone, it appeared, was now awake and watching her. She didn't smile. "Your attention, please."

A hush fell over the crowd. "We have a medical emergency and I desperately need antibiotics. Streptomycin, Levaquin, Avelox, Cipro—any kind of antibiotic but especially one of those four. Because of the storm, no one can get the medicine to me, and I can't get to it. If you have antibiotics, please speak up."

A few rows behind Briefcase Man, a disturbance broke out. An elderly man and woman arguing.

"Stop it, Ethan." The woman swatted at his hand, reaching for her purse.

Ethan glared at the woman and then spoke to Emma. "This is my wife, Claire. She's got antibiotics."

"And I'm keeping them, too." Claire pointed to her black-booted foot. "I had surgery. I need them."

Emma walked over to the woman. "Claire, you don't understand," Emma said softly. "I said it's an emergency. A child needs that medicine right now or she won't live."

"I need it, too."

Emma looked Claire over. "You don't appear to have had any surgical complications. Were there?"

"No, but I don't want any either."

"I understand. Honestly, I do." Emma resisted the urge to snatch her purse. "But this is a child, Claire, and I'm telling you, if she isn't treated with antibiotics, she will die."

Ethan urged his wife. "For land's sakes, give her the medicine, Claire."

"No." She frowned and spat at him. "I will not."

Short of forcibly taking the medicine from the woman, Emma wasn't going to get it.

Ethan gave his wife a look of pure disgust. "I can't believe you're the same woman I married. If I hadn't seen this myself, I wouldn't believe it."

Her eyes filled with tears. "I don't want to die."

"You've had surgery on your foot. You're not dying, but

even if you were, you've lived a whole life. This is a kid. A kid, Claire."

"Quit with your guilt. I mean it. I'm not giving her my medicine. I don't care what you or anyone else says. I'm not doing it."

Not even her husband's disgust softened Claire's resolve. Emma accepted it and tried a different tact. "Will you at least share it?"

Briefcase man, the gray-haired man Mason had vouched for, stepped forward. "Sharing won't be necessary," he told Emma. "I'm a doctor. I have what you need in my briefcase. You're welcome to it." He paused. "But I would like to see the patient. Perhaps I can help."

John Taylor nodded, then turned to the crowd. "Thank you, folks." He waved them back to whatever they had been doing. Ethan was welcomed by others in the group. Claire was not. She'd made her call, and she would now bear the consequences of it.

"Provided Dr. Martin agrees, your offer to help will be welcome," Emma told Briefcase Man.

Her eyes stretched wide, the look in them a little wild, Janette rushed over to Emma but spoke to John Taylor. "What is the medical emergency?"

"Excuse me a moment, doctor." Emma pivoted to face Janette and John Taylor. "Don't answer that, John Taylor," Emma interrupted, then focused on Janette. "The Security Chief is not at liberty to disclose that information." For good measure, she sent John Taylor a killer look. "Not one word or I'll have you prosecuted. Understand?"

"Yes, ma'am." He gave Janette a "you heard her" shrug.

"Take us back now, please, Chief," Emma added. "Doctor?" She motioned toward the alcove. "This way, please."

With every step, Emma prayed Mason had been right to trust this man. She felt torn on asking so much as the doctor's name. But he was a doctor, and if there was even a remote chance that he could help Olivia, they had to take it. They'd clear him first, of course.

John Taylor drove and wasted no time getting them back to the lab.

When he stopped the cart, Emma turned to the doctor. "You need to know that the child has been infected with a lethal pathogen. She's quarantined. Because her mother and brother were exposed to her, they're also quarantined."

He had kind eyes, and they were clear and met Emma's without surprise or hesitation. "Yes, I know."

Mason had to have told him. How else could the man possibly know? "And you're still willing to go in and see her? I could just take the medicine."

"I am willing. Actually, this is something I have to do."

He meant that literally. He was a man on a mission. But good or evil, she couldn't say. He appeared good, but even the most evil dregs in society never saw themselves as evil or bad. To them, they were just and reasonable and fair—even if they were psychotic or garden-variety nuts.

"Before you can go in, I have to get Dr. Martin to clear your access," she said. She snapped a photo of him then fired it off to Mason. *Grant Lab access?* A second text with the photo went to Liz. It included a single word message: *Identify*.

They left the cart and waited near the outer door for Mason's response.

Access granted.

"Okay, then," Emma said. "We're clear to go."

John Taylor looked uncertain if he should enter with them or return to the rear wall.

"You're good to go, John Taylor," Emma said, resolving his inner conflict. He might have doubted her before the encounter with Janette above, but he didn't now. "I've got this."

"Yes, ma'am. Radio me if you need me."

"Thanks." She entered the lab with the doctor.

Just inside, Mason stood waiting, expectant and clearly a little shocked. "Are you who I think—"

The doctor smiled and nodded. "I am a humbled man here to help, Dr. Mason," Briefcase Man said softly. "Don't make me regret it."

CHAPTER EIGHTEEN

Tuesday, December 18th
0628 (6:28 AM)

"Before I see the patient, we need to talk," the doctor said. "Is a parent of the child available? I'm assuming one of them works here or they wouldn't be here. Is that assumption correct?"

Certain he already knew the answer to that, Emma held her silence, waiting for Mason's response. It came immediately.

"David, the child's father, is my assistant," Mason said. "Both parents are here. Sophia is his wife, and the patient's mother. She's quarantined with her daughter, but we have two-way communications set up."

"The child is the patient—a girl, then?"

Mason nodded. "Olivia. Jacob, her little brother is also quarantined."

"I understand," the doctor said. "I expect Olivia needs her mother. Is David available?"

"I'm right here, doctor." David joined them. "There's fresh coffee in the kitchen. We can talk there."

David and the doctor walked down the hallway. Mason and Emma followed. "Are you going to fill me in?" she asked. "Who is this guy?"

"Later, I will." Mason glanced over at her. "I promise."

"I really shouldn't allow this, but these are desperate times, and Olivia's life is on the line. Know this, however. I am going to hold you to explaining, Mason." Emma studied his eyes. No secrets lurking in them, no shields hiding the truth. Both were good signs. "You're okay, right?"

He clasped her hand and gently squeezed. "I'm fine, Emma."

Her relief was sharp and immediate. And she didn't let go of his hand. The oddest thing was, he didn't seem to mind. Why? Because she'd trusted him?

In the kitchen, they sat at the table, their steaming hot mugs of coffee before them. "We need to bring your wife into the conversation," the doctor said. "Is there a way to do that without the children hearing what is said?"

"She has earbuds. We're already communicating privately."

Compassion lit the doctor's eyes. "This is difficult on all of you. I'm so sorry you're going through it."

The tone in his voice held the regret of one responsible. Why was that? Emma cut her gaze to Mason but found no answers there. Silent and stoic, he gave nothing away.

"So are we," David said. "But thank you for doing what you can to help." David paused a second to listen, as if Sophia was talking to him. Then, he asked, "How can you help?"

"I am Dr. Addison Cramer."

David and Mason recognized the name. They didn't bother trying to hide it. Emma didn't, but from their reaction, she knew Briefcase man was significant.

"I've worked with this pathogen." Cramer thumbed the rim of his cup. "For many years, I've been working on an antidote at a private facility." He looked to Emma. "I can't stress enough that it's critical to keep this pathogen contained."

Mason lowered his cup to the table. "We've done everything within our power, Dr. Cramer."

"I have a very limited supply of antidote."

Antidote? That was wonderful news! Limited supply... "How many doses?" Emma asked, hopeful for Olivia, worried about the others if the pathogen did go viral. "There are over five thousand people upstairs."

Dr. Cramer looked over at her. "Twelve."

Emma worried her lip. "That negates giving it until and unless symptoms appear."

"That's for the best, Emma," Dr. Cramer said, his expression sober.

"Why?"

"Is it really an antidote?" Mason asked. "Have you done clinical trials on it?"

"Only one," Dr. Cramer said. "He's sitting before you."

David bit back a groan that rumbled from deep in his throat. "You want to give my daughter a treatment that's been tried once. Only once?"

"Want to? No. No, I wish it were never needed for anyone. But done is done and we don't have much choice, David." Dr. Cramer said.

Emma cut in. "What about the typical antibiotics?"

He swiveled his head to look at her, his short beard all but hiding his flat-lined mouth. "They don't work, so there's no sense in endangering yourself or anyone else trying to get them."

"How do you know we're trying to get them?" she asked, deeply suspicious now.

"The same way I knew I needed to be here." He sipped

from his mug. Set it back down on the table. "I've been working on this project a long time," he said, looking at Mason. "I've tried every possible combination of every known drug, including several in the experimental phase." He paused to let Mason absorb the implications of that disclosure. "All failed."

Whether he worked for the CDC or David's people, she had no idea. But Dr. Cramer knew a lot more than he was telling any of them. And she suspected, his devotion to the project wasn't for some idle reason. Personal responsibility. Personal involvement had to be a key factor in his dedication to the project.

"Talk with your wife, David. Let me know if she has any questions. If I can answer, I will," Dr. Cramer said, then looked at Mason. "Dr. Martin—"

"Mason."

"Mason, can you brief me on the patient's current condition." Cramer wagged a finger in David's direction. "If Sophia hears anything that is no longer accurate, tell her to let us know right away."

David relayed the message, then relayed the conversation to Sophia. "Olivia is running a fever—102.9. She's suffering weakness, abdominal pain, and chills."

"No shock?" Dr. Cramer looked at David.

He nodded no.

Cramer looked back at Mason. "You have confirmed the diagnosis?"

"I have. Two tests. One in fluid, one in a tissue sample. Both test positive."

Dr. Cramer stilled. "May I see the test results?"

Mason looked at David. When he didn't respond, Mason said, "David, I've seen the results and Olivia. I believe without this treatment, she will die. I don't know all Dr. Cramer knows about this pathogen, but you've got to give permission for him to review the tests and examine Olivia. Do you and Sophia agree?"

David spoke softly to Sophia, then looked back at Mason and Dr. Cramer. "Go ahead," he said.

"This way, Dr. Cramer." Mason stood up.

Dr. Cramer paused. "David, I'll know more after reviewing the results and my examination."

David nodded, too emotional to speak.

Realizing he needed a minute to absorb all this and to talk to his wife, Emma too left the kitchen and stepped out into the tunnel to relay all she'd learned to Liz.

When Emma had, Liz told her, "I'll dig and see what I can find out. You don't sound totally comfortable with him showing up there."

"Would you be comfortable?" Emma asked. "I wouldn't trust him at all except Mason does." He'd been surprised to see the man, but not fearful of him. "I think he knew of him. And he remained very straightforward in the discussion about exactly what they were dealing with."

But the most telling part was that Mason didn't have to explain what BP7PP was. Cramer already knew. He had to have been a program insider to know that. The need to know loop was so small even Mason had trouble getting information on it.

A cart sped toward her. Emma positioned the rifle, in case it was needed. If four had escaped, that left one on the loose inside the facility, and he'd already killed Greer, which meant he had nothing to lose in killing again.

John Taylor flashed his lights, then stopped near Emma. "Figured you'd be out here, filing a report. You done?"

"Yes." She lowered her weapon. "What's the latest on the storm?"

"Raging. Janette just reported damage in the Main."

"How extensive is it?"

"She's relocating as many as she can to the other termi-nals, but they're packed to the rafters already. She wanted to bring them below. I shot that down."

"Did she listen to you?"

"I told her you'd vetoed it." He half-smiled. "I think she's a little scared of you."

The last thing Emma wanted was more people in closer proximity to the lab. "You didn't tell her about Greer, did you?"

"No. She saw the body. Ever since, she's been seeing phantoms of the shooter in every face," he said. "I don't have time to deal with more of that, so I told her the suspect had left the facility and the locals are in pursuit."

"But you didn't tell her it was a backup team."

"No way. She'd lose her mind."

"Agreed."

"I'm on my way up to check the damage." He hooked a thumb toward the elevator. "Janette said she has a construc-tion crew working on some shattered glass. No idea how bad it is. With her, anything that bumps the line on normal is a crisis."

"We'll hope it's minimal then."

"We've got a case of frostbite. Someone slipped outside to smoke and got locked out. There's a doctor in Terminal B taking care of him. Confirmed passenger."

"Good work, John Taylor."

"I wanted to check to make sure you're okay with this Dr. Cramer. I heard the early comms before you went into the kitchen to talk."

"Don't repeat his name. Not to anyone. Ever."

"Figured that. I heard his warning about being a guy trying to help and not making him regret it." John Taylor tapped at his glasses. "Any idea what that's all about?"

"Not a clue—yet." Emma said it and hated that it was true.

"It's not sitting right, this guy showing up with twelve doses of antidote," John Taylor said. "How do we know he isn't batting for the other side?"

"We don't. It's a risk." Mason had vouched for the man, but for Emma and John Taylor and people in their business, that alone wasn't enough. "But if we don't take it, Olivia dies."

"No choice, then." He grunted. "I'll let you know about the damage."

"Thanks."

John Taylor took off and soon disappeared from sight, and Emma returned to the lab.

On the screen into the quarantine room, Jacob stood watching Olivia.

Using sign language, she spoke to her brother. "Do not worry."

"Are you going to die, Liv?"

He sounded so vulnerable, so afraid. It opened a wound in Emma's chest.

"Someday." She sounded as frightened as he was, but also certain. And not defeated but positive. "But I'm not dying today." Not for a second did doubt creep into her voice.

"How do you know that?" Jacob asked her. "Bandit says he doesn't think you really know."

"Of course, I really know," Olivia insisted. "I asked for a Christmas miracle."

Oh, the fears that poured forth from Emma on hearing that threatened to send her staggering. If Olivia lived, it'd be a miracle. But if she didn't, her death would shatter Jacob's innocence. Emma prayed hard that wouldn't happen. Harder than she'd prayed for anything in a very long time.

Dr. Cramer had seen the exchange and he sniffed. "I don't even want to think of what happens if this doesn't work."

"Then make sure it does," Emma said. "I suspect you know more than anyone about this. Make it work. Do all you can to give Olivia and her family their Christmas miracle."

"I am trying, Emma. That's why I'm here. But I'm a mere mortal, not the Almighty."

"Sophia and many of us are praying for Him to intercede," Emma said. "You just do what you can."

Mason joined them. "Have you examined her already?"

"I've seen what I need to see in the tests. It's advanced."

David asked, "Will your antidote help her?"

"I wish I could say it positively would, but the truth is, I don't know, David." Dr. Cramer frowned, creasing the skin between his eyebrows. "Not this long after exposure. She'll be in shock in another hour." He turned to face David. "I'm afraid we have no choice. It's the untested antidote or Olivia will certainly die before the end of the day."

David gulped in a ragged breath, then started to share that information with Sophia, but she cut him off. "Do it," he relayed word from his wife.

Dr. Cramer paused. "You both agree?"

"There's no choice. With it, she has a chance to live. Without it, she dies."

"David, this has never been given to a child." Compassion and brutal honesty burned in Cramer's eyes. "You must understand. It could also kill her."

David blinked hard, cleared his throat. "Then let me go in with you."

Dr. Cramer nodded, then whispered to Emma. "Know that I've been praying for divine assistance on this every day since . . . every day. It's a miracle I've gotten this far. I'm daring to believe for another miracle."

"So am I." Emma whispered. He walked on and Emma stood board stiff, watching the monitor until the men entered the quarantine room.

"You okay?" Mason slipped an arm around her shoulder.

"Honestly?" Emma leaned against him and tilted her head against his chest. "No, Mason. I'm not okay."

"Have faith." He dropped a kiss to the crown of her head. "I hope he talks to Olivia first. She hates shots. Fears the needle."

"What?" Emma pulled back and looked at Mason.

"Doctors who spend all their time in the lab don't tend to have good bedside manners. We're not used to them."

"I'm sure he'll be good." Feeling responsible for Olivia being there and in this position, of course, he would be good.

"I hope so," Mason said. "Olivia is always the strong one. The one who knows the answers and takes care of everyone else, especially Jacob. He'd be lost without her."

Emma rubbed Mason's arm. "Olivia strikes me as a very determined girl. She told Jacob she wasn't going to die today. She's asked for a Christmas miracle."

"I hope she gets it," Mason said. "I can't imagine losing her."

Emma hugged him hard. "Don't. Focus on imagining her surviving."

Mason gathered and held Emma in his arms. "I always could count on you to look at things through the right lens, Emma."

She clasped her hands around his waist. "You never paid attention to a word I said."

"You're wrong about that." He pulled back and smiled down at her. "I saw you in everything. Heard you in everything. Nothing about you escaped me."

"Then why did you ignore me?"

"Buffet."

She rolled her eyes. "One day, I'm going to explain what that's all about to you." She just had to make sure she was right about it before she did it.

"I look forward to it."

"He's in there with Olivia," Emma warned.

Mason turned and clasped her hand, not willing yet to let go.

As they stood and watched, Dr. Cramer talked to Olivia, listened to her mother, talked some more. After a few minutes, he explained the injection, then asked if Olivia was ready.

"I've been waiting for you," she said. "You seemed upset when you first got here, but I think you're a little better now. Are you?"

"I am," he said. "Thank you for being patient with me."

"It's scary, but it'll be okay."

He cleared his throat. His Adam's apple bobbed. "So, you're ready then?"

"One second." She smiled at her mother. "I love you."

"I love you, too, honey." Sophia smiled, but silent tears streamed down her face.

David stood beside Sophia, and Olivia focused on him. "Love you, Daddy."

"Love you, too." He smiled. "You're very brave, Liv. I'm so proud of you."

Olivia turned her head on the pillow. "Jacob, remember what I told you. Not today."

"I won't forget." He squeezed Bandit. "Christmas miracle."

"That's right." She nodded, then looked at Dr. Cramer. "I'm ready now."

Emma felt her face, surprised to find it wet with tears.

Mason dried them with his hand, ignoring his own. "It's going to be okay, Emma."

"It will, right? I mean, she's too headstrong to die on a day she said she wouldn't."

"It wouldn't surprise me a bit." He dropped a kiss to her

forehead. "Olivia would never lie to Jacob. He totally trusts her, and she would never do anything to jeopardize that. It's probably the best thing going for her."

"Dr. Cramer, you tried your hardest. I know that, okay?" Olivia said.

"Thank you, Olivia." His voice cracked.

She was brave, Emma thought. Maybe the bravest person Emma had ever known. Surrounded by people covered in shields and masks and scrubs—everyone, except for her, and she'd made sure to say words that would sustain and comfort them no matter what happened. Even in this, Olivia was reassuring them. Maybe that's how she reassured herself and stayed strong. And she was nine. Only nine. One day, she would be a formidable woman. She was already an amazing girl, wise beyond her years.

"There. All done." Dr. Cramer withdrew the needle. "Now, if anything feels funny, you let me know right away." He pulled a chair close to her bedside and sat down.

Olivia watched him with unabashed interest. "You're staying in here with me?"

"I am," Dr. Cramer said and grinned. "You're too much fun not to be around."

She smiled, though it was droopy. "What do we do now?"

"We wait," the doctor said. "And we pray."

CHAPTER NINETEEN

"Well, she survived the injection," Mason said, his fisted hands buried deep in his lab jacket pockets.

"That's a good sign." Emma backed away from the monitor. "Now if it just works." She looked up at Mason, seeking reassurance. They'd taken a big leap of faith on Cramer, and Mason seemed comfortable with it. For Olivia's sake, Emma hoped that hadn't been a mistake. "How long until we know?"

Uncertainty flickered across Mason's face, mingled with the worry. "These are uncharted waters, Emma."

"You know Dr. Cramer or you'd never have agreed to this," she said. "I need to know how, who he is, and—"

"That can wait," Mason said, firmly shutting that door. At least, for now. "Did you find the invaders?"

"One is loose in the facility. John Taylor and his team are searching." She looked over at the inner hub, grateful there were no alarms. The system lights were all blissfully green.

"Four of them escaped in a black van with diplomatic plates on it."

"You saw that?"

"John Taylor picked it up off of the facility security cameras," she said. "Liz has alerted the authorities. The storm makes it harder for those trying to flee."

"And for those trying to pursue them," Mason said. "It's not good news that they've got diplomatic status."

"No, it isn't. But we created a workaround on that and it's in place." Emma reached for a tissue and dabbed at her eyes. They burned like fire due to all the irritants in the tunnels.

"Thanks to the storm, they've got nowhere to go, and no way to get there," he said, then wiggled a fingertip. "What's going on with your eyes?"

His concern touched her. She tilted her head, hoping he wouldn't notice. "They've been open too long."

"You're welcome to rest in my quarters."

The temptation to take him up on that was great, but unwise. "Maybe later. John Taylor might need an extra set of hands."

"His staff is efficient, or they wouldn't work for him."

"He is skilled. I'm surprised he hasn't been recruited by an urban facility."

"Many have tried. He won't leave Portal. He used to work in Miami. But then his daughter was kidnapped while waiting for the school bus. That changed everything," Mason said.

"I'm sure it did." A parent's worst nightmare. "What happened to her?"

"John Taylor found her before she could be trafficked and moved the family here."

"Thank goodness for that." How relieved he must have been. "Why come here?"

Mason nodded. "John Taylor was raised in Portal."

"So he came home, where he felt his family would be safe."

"I think that was it exactly." Mason sighed. "I can't see him leaving here until his daughter is an adult and on her own."

Emma's skin crawled. "Horrific event, but what a blessing that he found her and got her back."

"It was," Mason agreed. "He doesn't like to talk about it, but every once in a while, he'll hear about a case. He takes a couple days off and joins the search."

"Tell me he enjoys some success."

"He does. He has a keen insight on it. Takes calls and offers opinions even when he can't physically be there. To be honest, after his daughter leaves home, I expect he'll devote himself full-time to recovering trafficked victims. He's said as much half a dozen times."

"Takes a lot of resolve and nerves of steel to do that kind of work." Emma gazed again at the green lights. "I hope he's incredibly successful."

"So do I. People that traffic kids..." Mason's mouth flattened and he didn't finish his statement. "Anyway, he demands a lot from his staff, and they deliver, or he weeds them out. They're familiar with every inch of this facility. It's probably best for you to rest a while and leave them to it. They'll know if something has changed or is out of place."

"I can't do that. Two backup teams got in," she reminded Mason. "They nearly blew us all to kingdom come."

"Ten people in a flood of five thousand."

"True. But it only takes one to set off a blast that could create a pandemic." She visibly shuddered. "The thought of that scares me awake."

"It does me, too." He clasped her shoulder. "Occupational hazard. The ones dealing with Holly think it's the most pressing and dangerous thing going. And it is pressing and dangerous. But those of us who know about the risks for a pandemic... Well, there's no peace to be had until the threat is eliminated." Mason extended a hand to her. "So, we can't sleep, but let's at least go sit down for a few minutes."

Emma clasped his hand, took comfort in his fingers closing around hers, in the pressing together of their palms. They walked down the hallway to the far end of the kitchen. Two sofas and a smattering of chairs were arranged around a television set. It was on and tuned into the local weather, but the sound was muted.

Leaving it muted, Emma sat down on the sofa and sank into its cushions.

Mason sat beside her. He had that look. The one that warned her something was on his mind and he wanted to talk about it. She was content to not prod him. Just to sit and wait and let him get around to it. He would, after he'd sorted it all out in his mind and knew what he wanted to say.

Minutes passed with him staring blankly at the TV screen. Then a few more minutes went by and finally he looked over at her. "I think I've been wrong about you, Emma."

Was that a good or a bad thing? She didn't have a clue. "How so?"

"For a long time, I thought you were flighty. You know, that you had no idea what you wanted or needed, and that's why you went through so many guys. But you're not flighty at all. You're a very deliberate person, and capable of a lot of things. I had this whole image of you that was wrong. No way around that. I'm sorry I misjudged you."

"Thank you for telling me." She shrugged a shoulder. "Normally, I don't pay much attention to what other people think. I care intensely what I think, and I know my motivations. But with you, even for me...it's different."

"Why is that?"

She considered sidestepping his question. But isn't that what got them into the world of misunderstandings they lived in now? How she managed, she wasn't sure, but she met his eyes. "Because what you think matters, Mason. You matter. You always have."

"So do you." He sighed, as if relieved to finally say that aloud. "We've known each other a long time, but I've learned more about you since you've been here than I ever knew about you before."

"You saw what you expected to see." She sniffed. "I get that."

"The buffet line obscured my view?"

There was no missing the self-recrimination in his tone. "Something like that."

He frowned. "I really am sorry, Emma. I should have asked you about something before, but I thought I already knew the answer. I didn't. I see that clearly now."

"Go ahead and ask me." The sooner they ended the misunderstandings and misconceptions, the better. "But know that you might not like the answer." She hoped that wouldn't be the case. They were making progress. Still, it might. Her mouth went dry. She swallowed hard, steeled herself, hoping neither of them would be disappointed.

"In school, you went through a lot of guys. Since then, you've been engaged several times, but you didn't marry any of them."

"I've been engaged twice," she corrected him. "And I didn't marry either of them."

He dipped his chin and didn't look directly at her. "May I ask why not?"

She didn't hedge, and hoped that wouldn't be a regret she had to lug around, too. "Everyone thought it was poor judgment. That I'd jump into dating or getting engaged, and then realize I'd jumped prematurely."

He did look at her then. "Honestly, before the last couple days, that's exactly what I thought."

She frowned at him. "It wasn't that."

"I've already said I was wrong and apologized."

He had. "My judgment is sound," she assured Mason. "To a man, I thought I could care about each one of them. So, I invested. But then I didn't. Care, I mean." She sighed and draped a hand on her thigh. "Don't get me wrong. Many of them were really good men."

"Not all of them."

"True, there were a couple of losers in the bunch, but for the most part, they were decent guys. Just not guys I could care about. You know what I mean."

"Actually, I don't." Mason puzzling over this in his mind played out in his expression. "It doesn't make sense."

She hiked a shoulder. "It makes perfect sense to me."

"Sorry, I'm trying but I'm not tracking you."

She sat up straight, curled her fingers and fisted her hand on her thigh. "Imagine knowing exactly what you want and searching for it. You think you find it, and so you invest. Of course, it isn't exactly what you wanted, and so you think, that's okay. It's close. Close is enough. Nothing is ever exactly perfect, you know? But close can be good. So, you deal with it."

He rubbed at his chin. "And that works for a while, only you can't keep dealing with it."

"Exactly." She lifted a hand, relived that he was following along. "You start seeing the differences and they become more and more defined and clear and sharp, and pretty soon you wonder what you were thinking to even imagine that this guy or that one was close enough to what you wanted for anything to ever work between you."

Mason nodded. "That's when you'd end it."

"Yes." He really was getting it. "I didn't want to settle, so I'd end it."

"Okay, I get that. Really, I do. But over and over again?"

"I'm afraid so," she said without apology. "If the differences had all been in one way, it wouldn't have taken so many times. But they weren't what I wanted in different ways. Men aren't like a salad, Mason, where you can pick and choose what goes in. It takes time to figure out what all is in the bowl. Sometimes, you can figure out fast, and other times, well, it takes a while."

"The engagements took the longest to figure out."

"They did. But I don't regret them." She looked over at him. "Better to break an engagement than to marry and divorce. Though, after my own experience, I have a lot of empathy for those on that front, too."

He digested all that for a long minute. "So, who did you want?"

That unexpected question rattled her. "Excuse me?"

"You said you knew exactly what you wanted." He tilted his head. "I'm assuming you had a man in mind that was the model for that. Who was he?"

Too fast. He wasn't ready to hear it, and she wasn't ready to reveal it. She was maxed out on vulnerabilities right now. "Someone else." Finally, after all this time of not understanding what she'd been doing herself, on seeing Mason again and talking with him now in such earnest, she understood perfectly. "And you? Why aren't you married—or are you?"

"No, I'm not."

Her heart dropped from her throat back into her chest where it belonged. "Have you ever been married?"

He avoided looking at her. "No."

"No desire, fear of commitment, or what?"

"No fear. I came close once, but it didn't work out."

"You were engaged?" Emma pressed him.

"Not that close. But I did consider it."

"Why didn't it work out?"

He grunted. "She wasn't who I thought she was."

"That sounds familiar." Emma actually smiled. "I totally understand that."

"I guess you would." He smiled back at her and a lovely little twinkle lit in his eyes. "I definitely misjudged you, Emma."

"All these years?"

"Maybe. Definitely for most of them."

She worried her lower lip with her teeth. "I think that's the nicest thing you've ever said to me."

He flushed. "I'm sorry about that, too." He scooted closer and turned toward her. "I've wanted to do something for a long, long time. I was advised against it, but a proper apology requires a forgiveness kiss. Don't you agree?"

Her heart beat hard and fast. "It does in my world." Emma leaned into him and they kissed, gently, tenderly exploring...and Mason's radio blared.

"Dr. M.? Dr. Martin? Are you reading me?"

He fished the radio from his waist and responded. "David? What's up?"

"You need to get in here. Dr. Cramer says Olivia is in dangerous territory."

"What can I do?"

"She's been vaccinated."

"I know. Emma and I watched on the monitor." Mason frowned his confusion, stood up, and cut to the chase. "What's Cramer saying on time? How long until we know whether or not the antidote is going to work?"

"An hour," David said. "Maybe a little longer, but not much." David hesitated. "We need a little miracle, Dr. M."

Emma wished she had one to give him.

"Hang on and stay calm so you don't upset Sophia and the kids. I'll be right there." Mason's tone softened and he held Emma's gaze. "And, David, remember that miracles happen every day."

Emma loved that. Her weariness faded and her spirits soared. His words inspired her.

And then the power went out.

CHAPTER TWENTY

Tuesday, December 18th
    0712 (7:12 AM)

"Don't panic," Mason told Emma. "Power's down, but the auxiliary backup generators will come online any moment."

Thirty seconds later, the power came up, and the lights came on.

"Okay, then." Brushing a hand across her forehead, Emma smiled, deeply relieved. "That wasn't fun. But we can work with this."

Mason remained tense. "Not fun at all." He headed toward the hallway. "I need to get to Olivia."

Emma followed. She needed to check in with John Taylor, and make sure the blackout hadn't resulted in pandemonium above or on the rear wall. She pulled out her radio. "Security Chief. Miller paging Security Chief."

"Go ahead, Emma."

Loud crackling noises sounded in the background, and a steady hum of chatter. "Where are you?"

"Rear wall. Upstairs is lit. Janette and staff are calming people down."

On alert, Emma strained to identify the sounds, but couldn't peg them. "What's the crackling noise I'm hearing?"

"I'm having the construction crew cover the rear wall with tarps and duct tape." He grunted. "It isn't ideal, but it seems prudent since we're on auxiliary power."

It did. "Good call," she said. "I'm on my way down there."

"Emma, right before the power went down," John Taylor said, "I took out our loose cannon."

The invader. She paused her steps to fully focus. "What happened?"

John Taylor said, "Just a second."

Mason overheard the conversation and stopped. She waved him to go on. "I've got this," she mouthed.

He nodded and then took the turn to the gear station set up outside Olivia's room. He'd suit up and shield before entering her room.

Emma walked on toward the outer door, snagging the rifle on her way. Two steps from the outer door, the power went off, plunging them into pitch black darkness.

"Emma!" Mason's voice echoed down the hallway to her.

"I'm fine, Mason. I've got to go to the rear wall." She needed to gather info and evidence on the invader fatality and file a report with Liz.

"Okay."

Sliding her fingers along the wall, she came to the door frame and stopped. "Can I get out of here with the power out?"

"The door has a battery backup," Mason called back. "Punch in one and then the code."

She felt for the pad and tapped what she hoped was the one key. The keypad lit up, piercing the darkness. Relieved, she yelled to Mason. "Going."

"Be careful."

Satisfaction swam through her. He cared. He might not care in the way she wished he would, but he wasn't immune to her. The deep freeze was starting to thaw. She spoke into the radio. "John Taylor, is all power down now?"

"Yes, ma'am. Facility wide."

"Is the suspect dead?"

"Yeah, he is. I had no choice, Emma. He drew down on me."

That knocked out a lot of potential problems. "Where did it happen?"

"In the tunnel, about ten yards from the back wall. I was on foot staked out in there. I tracked him, to get a fix on if there were more of them and how they were getting in. He stopped in the tunnel and started rifling through his gear, putting something together. I surprised him."

"What was he putting together?" Had to be a charge. Had to be. He'd do the prep work protected by the tunnel. Set the charge in place and finish up at the rear wall. Less time out in the open, vulnerable. Aided by her flashlight, she made her way to the cart.

"Getting ready to set off another charge. I interrupted him."

"He wasn't successful." Speculating, but any blast would have been heard and likely felt in the lab.

"No, he wasn't. But I'll feel better once you take a look and undo what he was doing."

Emma took off down the tunnel. "What about the guys? None of them interacted with him?"

"I radioed for them to stand down and stay out of sight."

So that he could maybe learn how they were coming in and how many of them were here. John Taylor was very good. Very good. "Did you or any of them see anyone else?"

"No, ma'am. Not a soul."

"And none of our guys were hurt?"

"Not a one."

"Well done, John Taylor." The tunnel split. Emma veered left. "I'm on my way now. Make sure no one gets anywhere near the charge or the body."

"It's taped off and I've got men standing guard on both locations."

"The fatality," she said, gripping the wheel. "You're sure he was alone? No doubt, right?"

"Yeah, he was alone." John Taylor cleared his throat. "I think he was one of the five backup team. We know the other four got away. At least, from the facility. I'm monitoring the locals and their APB is out on the van. The police chief knows what's up, and they're all over it. Well, as much as they can be with Holly raging out there."

Blasted storm was making a difficult task even harder. "Is the storm still parked over us, or what?"

"Pretty much stalled out, according to Darcy Keller."

Not the news Emma wanted to hear. "Be there shortly. Keep a sharp watch."

"You, too, Emma. Chief out."

She drove as fast as she dared, seeing nothing and no one else. When she neared the segment of tunnel leading to the rear wall chamber, she slowed down and phoned Liz, filled her in on developments, then ended with, "Get headquarters on this power outage, Liz. Fast. Or we could be facing a national nightmare the likes of which this country has never seen."

EMMA PHOTOGRAPHED the dead man by flashlight. Dressed like the others, he was just as well-equipped as they had been and just as indistinguishable. He could be from anywhere, really. That was the thing with CAR. The organization didn't care who it dealt with or where they were from so long as their eyes were on the bottom line. There was no ideology or national interest involved, only money. The more of it, the better. Greed never shone more brightly or revealed more ugliness.

She forwarded the man's photo to Liz with photos of the charge. He hadn't gotten very far on the charge before he'd been interrupted. She disposed of the problem with little effort, then secured the explosives and went in search of John Taylor.

Emma found him at the lab's rear wall. He stood, hands on hips, watching the crew stretch and duct tape black tarps over the area with the sealed cracks.

Emma joined him. "Hey."

"You gather the evidence you need in the tunnel?" John Taylor kept his gaze on the work being done by the crew. "Get the device disassembled?"

"Yes, on both. All safe and secure. Your men can remove the body." No doubt he'd put it in the storage area where the others had been placed. Only Greer had been in a different location. Emma understood the respect being shown to Greer in keeping his body separate from those of the thugs. After the storm, when the coroner could get in to retrieve the bodies, he would understand, too.

John Taylor made a call on his radio and ordered the body moved.

The crew had set up battery-powered lights in the opening between the lab's rear wall and the jagged hole open to the outside. It was cooler, of course, but the area didn't look that much different than it had when the power was on. "Are there more of these lights? Might come in handy upstairs."

John Taylor spoke to a member of a second construction crew above. He too had a radio and put out a call.

When John Taylor walked back to Emma, he said, "They're putting them in place now. Maybe that will calm down Janette and get her off my back for more than five minutes."

Emma nodded, though they both doubted anything could keep Janette off his back right now. Her plan to snatch her boss's job had hit a few unexpected snags. She was in deep, doing damage control and seeking something to salvage that promotion. It wasn't happening. Her people didn't trust her. Trust was key to passenger and facility protection. If Emma had to intercede, she would. Honestly, it shouldn't come to that. "The tarps will help keep moisture out," Emma said. "That's good."

"Praying it keeps germs in, too. If it holds, with a little luck, this whole area won't be contaminated." He slid her a worried look. "If it is, it will spread, Emma. No two ways about it."

It would, and that would be devastating. "You realize the air isn't being cleaned in the HC lab." When John Taylor nodded, she added, "Mason might have some good advice for us." Emma pulled out her radio and called him, told him about the tarps, and verified the air still wasn't being cleaned.

"That's right, it's not," he said. "Without power, the temperature will rise quickly, and the pathogens will be active."

"Kill them now, then." Emma lifted a hand. "You've got the equipment." He had used it earlier to kill the pathogens outside the freezer and the damaged vial in the HC's inner hub.

"I can't," Mason said. "I have the equipment, but I don't have the ability to use it."

"You need power to do it." Emma's stomach fluttered. Of course, he did.

"Yes." He confirmed it. "The rear wall is most vulnerable." Mason mentally worked through it, then continued. "The freezers will hold for at least eight hours, provided that wall doesn't heat up."

Emma thought about it. "We can ice the freezers."

"No, you can't," he said. "First, you'd have to reveal the lab is here and what's in it. Secondly, the melting ice would be contaminated, and we can't seal it in the lab. If we open the lab to the traffic required to pack it, we won't have eight hours. Off the top of my head, I'd say three hours, max. We can't lose that much time."

Emma regrouped, realigned her thinking. "What about icing the outer rear wall? We can cool it down. The cracks have been sealed and the crew's putting tarps up now."

"Affixed with?"

"Duct tape." Her mother used to insist duct tape was as essential in every home as a skillet. Emma prayed that was so and not a tale. There had been many occasions growing up when it had been used and had made all the difference. "Will packing the wall help? Heaven knows, we've got plenty of snow and ice outside." If it melted, and there was no leak, it'd cause no harm.

"Actually, that's a good idea."

Motivated by good news, Emma almost smiled. Almost. "The construction crew guarding the area will help. If they can get to the heavy equipment, it can be done rapidly, too."

"The sooner the better. While the lab is still cold." Mason sounded more hopeful. "But whatever is done, do not break the seal into the HC, Emma."

What was in those freezers could wipe out the people in the facility in hours, the state in days, and within two weeks, the entire country. "I understand."

"David!" Sophia shouted out. "David, do you hear me?"

Emma stilled. "What's going on? Is it Olivia? Is she getting worse?"

"I'm not sure," Mason said. "Hold on."

David's background voice carried over the radio. "Sophia, what's going on?"

"It's Olivia. David, it's Olivia!"

"What about her, Sophia?" Mason called out.

Emma held her breath. Tensed all over. Sophia sounded frantic. Excited. Ecstatic. But she did not sound desperate or devastated. Emma dared to hope, prodded Mason. "Is she—"

"Hold on, Emma," he said again. "I don't know yet..."

The revelation burst from Sophia. "Her fever broke!"

Oh, that had to be good news. Didn't that have to be good news? "Does this mean—" Emma started.

Mason laughed. "It's the best of signs. The antidote is killing the pathogen."

"She is going to be all right." Tears welled in Emma's eyes. She blinked hard and swallowed a lump that hung in her throat. "That's what it means, right?"

"I suspect that's exactly what it means," Mason sounded thrilled. "I'm seeking confirmation from Dr. Cramer. Hang tight."

A long, tense minute passed. Then another. Finally, Mason came back to the radio. "Dr. Cramer confirmed it. She's going to make it, Emma." Mason was so happy, his buoyant voice filled with laughter and heartfelt relief. "Olivia is going to live!"

"That's wonderful news. The best news ever." Emma slumped, then laughed. "John Taylor," she shouted out. "She's going to live!"

Word spread quickly among the men. Spontaneous cheers, back-slapping and laughter erupted in the construction crew. To a man, they knew exactly what this meant. They too would survive. John Taylor would survive to continue to protect his daughter.

Emma too would survive.

It had been abundantly clear. If one of them died, likely all of them would, and they had known it from the start. Elated they all would live, Emma smiled into the radio. "Mason, do you hear that?"

"I do."

Emma dragged her teeth over her lower lip. "I wish I could see Jacob's face right now." That she had upset him earlier had been preying on her ever since.

"He's wondering what all the hoopla is about. Olivia said she wasn't dying today. In his eyes, that was the final authority on the matter. So, why's everybody surprised? She said she would live and she did." Mason chuckled.

Emma loved Jacob's matter-of-fact faith and innocence. Her lips curved into a smile when what she really wanted to do was weep her relief. "You know, Mason, sometimes life is so good."

"It is," he agreed. "Though I have to say, you're a strange woman, to be in your current position and saying that, Emma."

"Not strange at all."

Mason dropped his voice low. "I love how your mind works."

"Yeah, it's a real wonder."

To the sounds of his laughter, she shut down the radio.

CHAPTER TWENTY-ONE

TUESDAY, December 18ᵗʰ
1122 (11:22 AM)

EVEN WITH HEAVY EQUIPMENT, it took hours to get the snowpack in place against the rear wall. When it was done, the crew looked ready to fall over. They'd been without rest for nearly forty-eight hours, and under extreme duress. Signs of exhaustion were all over them.

John Taylor met up with Emma near the mouth of the tunnel. "Power is down for the duration of the storm." He spoke softly. "As soon as visibility improves, they'll begin clearing the roads and get backup established. It's first priority."

"Is there good news on the storm front?" Emma asked.

"There is. Holly isn't parked on our heads anymore. Slow, but it is finally moving again."

"Thank heaven for that." Emma couldn't wait for this storm to move on.

Two carts drove toward them. When they stopped, a

woman about forty wearing a smudged apron got out and walked over to John Taylor. "Hey," she said. "We figured you guys had to be half-starved. It's just pizza, but it'll fill stomachs."

Thanks, Sam," John Taylor told the woman. Her uniform looked about as tired as Emma's dusty clothes, but Sam had a spring in her step. "We've been going at it making as many of these as we can. We weren't stocked to feed this many people, but we're all making do, trying our best."

"We all appreciate your efforts, Sam," he said. "I know the guys will really be happy."

She motioned to two women sitting in the carts to deliver the pizza, then focused on Emma. "You did a good job above with the people, getting the medicine for the child."

"Thank you." Emma turned the topic. "This was thoughtful of you and your people, Sam, to bring food down to the guys. I know they're hungry."

"We have to look out for each other as best we can. In trying times, people have to stick together, you know?"

Emma smiled. "I do."

"We heard about the little girl on the way down. That she's going to be okay." Sam looked relieved. "Glad to hear that."

"We're hopeful," Emma said. "Her fever has broken, and they say that's a great sign."

"Lucky that doctor was here, and he had antibiotics."

"Yes, we sure were." Emma was being pumped for information for the gossip mill but sensed no ill will in it. She borrowed a phrase from Olivia. "It's a Christmas miracle."

"Rates as one in my book." Sam turned and headed back to the cart. "A little good news lifts everyone's heart."

"Couldn't agree more." Emma smiled at her and added a wave.

John Taylor waited until Sam was out of earshot. "Claire,

the woman who wouldn't share her antibiotics, isn't faring too well."

Emma slid her focus to John Taylor. "What's wrong with her?"

"No one will sell her food or anything to drink."

"Because she wouldn't share her medicine?"

John Taylor nodded. "My guys asked if they should take her something."

Emma sent him a curious look. "What did you tell them?"

"To give the woman food and drink." He shrugged. "She's recovering from surgery, and... It's just the right thing to do."

"It is the right thing to do, John Taylor."

"I was a little worried you wouldn't approve."

"No, I think you did exactly the right thing. We have to treat others as we would want them to treat us, not as they do. Be a good example. My mother used to say, you can't control how others behave, but you do control how you behave. Both of you must answer for your behavior."

"Our folks went to the same school." John Taylor laughed. "You never let anyone go hungry if you can help it." He gazed off. "When my daughter was missing, a stranger helped her. I'll never forget it."

So, he helped others to repay the kindness done to help his daughter. That moved Emma. She swallowed a lump rising in her throat. "She's a lucky girl. And so are those you help, John Taylor." Emma cleared her throat. "I think your folks would be really proud of the man you've become." Emma pointed to the ice-packed wall. "Keep that frozen as best you can."

"Yes, ma'am. We're on it."

Emma glanced at the guys kicking back drinks and pizza. Talking, laughing. It was a beautiful thing. They'd come down here in an act of courage, bent on doing all they could to save the lives of others. To spare their families, if they could. And they'd done it knowing they could be called on to make the ultimate sacrifice. They were heroes. One and all. Heroes.

Emma climbed into the cart, tired but hopeful, seeing the good in a lot of people, and feeling a lot better about their situation than she had hours earlier. If the seals held and the pathogens stayed put in the freezers and they remained inactive, they all might just survive Holly.

She drove back to the lab and, in the outer ring, hung her rifle on the hook, then went straight to the monitors. Still in bed, Olivia looked weak, and Emma supposed she was, but her color was already better, and Jacob was dangling Bandit by a paw.

That was the best sign that things were improving. He wasn't clutching Bandit to his throat with his face buried in the pup's scruff.

Mason came down the hall. On seeing her, he smiled. "You're back. How did the snowpack work out?"

"Good, so far. Is it helping in here?"

He checked the monitors, then a thermostat. "We're still below freezing, so I'd say, yes. If we don't have to go in before power returns, with what you've done, we should be okay."

"The guys have done the work." Relief settled her stomach. "Do we need to ice the front wall, too?" she asked. It would expose the lab, but exposure beat the socks off being dead to avoid exposure.

"Not now," Mason said. "For now, we're good. We'll watch it. If we see the temperature rising, we'll reconsider."

"Works for me." With just David and Mason and her, and maybe John Taylor, hauling the ice from the tunnel to the inner front wall, it'd be a major job, especially without the benefit of heavy equipment.

"Where's Dr. Cramer?" He wasn't in the quarantine room. She scanned but saw no signs of him on any of the monitors.

Mason frowned. "I'm not sure. He was here just a minute ago."

Emma checked the monitors again. Cramer wasn't anywhere in the lab. "He's gone," she said, then looked over at Mason. "Did he take the antidote with him?"

"No. It's locked in the fridge," Mason assured her. "I put it in there myself." He passed her a fresh flashlight. "Maybe he went upstairs to get something to eat. He's not fond of spaghetti. That and scrambled eggs is about all I'm good at. I made more spaghetti."

"With Sophia's sauce?" Emma asked. The rich smell of it wafted down the hall.

"It's the best." Mason smiled. "I'm starved."

Emma's stomach had been growling for hours. "I need fuel, too."

"Then, let's eat." He started toward the kitchen.

"I'll be right there." Emma swiped her hair back from her face. She'd give her front teeth for a hot shower. And toss in two molars for a shampoo. But power was required for that, too. "I need to report in first."

EMMA STOOD JUST beyond the outer door of the lab and phoned Liz.

"Good timing. I was about to call you," Liz said. "We just heard from headquarters and they've verified the identity of the man in the last photo you sent—the invader John Taylor took out who was trying to set off another blast. He's directly connected to CAR. His name wasn't released to us, but headquarters did confirm the connection. The think tank there is confident this attack isn't terror-related, so to speak, but is CAR trying to get its hands on the pathogen to sell on the black-market."

Expected. But confirmation was good news. The invaders' intent wasn't to infect people in a mass incident attack. The bad news? They wanted to steal the pathogen so others who would infect people in a mass incident attack could. Greedy thugs. "We knew it. With CAR, it's always about the money."

"Exactly," Liz agreed. "But we got a break there, so I'm grateful for it. And they didn't get the pathogen, and I'm really grateful for that."

"True on both counts." Emma leaned back against the lab door.

"Um," Liz said, hesitating. "I'm almost scared to ask, but I need to know. Can I take it that your calm means Olivia is still with us?"

"She is still with us, and her fever has broken." Emma shined the flashlight down the tunnel. It was clear. "Mason says, it appears as if she's going to recover."

"That's great news. I know you were worried. Everyone was worried."

"Olivia wasn't," Emma said. "She told her little brother she wouldn't die today."

"How could she know that?"

"She says, she asked for a Christmas miracle. And she said that Dr. Cramer told her she'd gotten one." Emma paused, rubbed at her temple. "Actually, he is why I'm calling. He's dropped off the radar."

"Interesting."

"Very," Emma said. "Olivia said, right after her fever broke, he told her she was going to be fine and he left the quarantine room. That's the last anyone's seen of him."

"And Dr. Hunk hasn't told you anything about him?"

"Beyond confirming the man's name being Addison Cramer, not really."

Liz's voice spiked higher. "Did you say Addison Cramer?"

"I did, yes."

"Are you sure? Before, you just told me Dr. Cramer. You're sure it was Addison?"

"Addison Cramer. Yes, I'm sure. That's how he identified himself." Emma didn't like the edge in Liz's tone. It set off alarms in her that were never a good sign.

"But that's impossible, Emma."

"Why?"

"Because Addison Cramer not only worked on developing BP7PP, he ran the entire program."

"Okay." Emma wasn't yet connecting why that made it impossible for him to show up here. Actually, it made it more likely.

"He agreed to develop BP7PP because of the Russian's Small Pox event. But he insisted he'd develop BP7PP only if he was allowed to develop the antidote to it simultaneously. The honchos agreed."

Emma still wasn't tracking. "So, what is the conflict?" She lifted a hand. "Is there one?"

"Oh, yeah. There is. And it's a big one."

Was Liz going to share it or just taunt Emma? "Well?"

"When the weaponized version of the pathogen was done," Liz said, "the antidote still wasn't working. Dr. Cramer needed more time and money."

The conflict smacked into Emma. She swallowed a gasp. "They shut down the program on him."

"Yes!"

Emma's mind whirled. "He said he went to a private facility and continued to work on the antidote there."

"But see, that's impossible, Emma," Liz insisted.

Impossible. Not unlikely, but impossible. "Why?"

"Because Addison Cramer committed suicide the same day that they shut down the project."

Shock coursed through Emma. "What? You're telling me Dr. Cramer is dead?"

"Dead and buried."

"Well, he looked pretty healthy for a corpse, and Mason recognized him." She recalled the exact exchange. "He said he was a man here to help and not to make him regret it. He'd been hanging out in the airport for three days."

"The project ended June 12, 2010. Addison Cramer died June 12, 2010."

"So, if he's dead, then who was here?" Emma asked.

"And what did he give Olivia?" Liz answered with a question of her own.

"I don't know, but whatever it was, it worked." Emma had believed him. She had trusted Mason. "Cramer couldn't have died. It had to have been him. Who else would have that kind of insight and information on the pathogen?"

"I'm not sure, but I'd say your Dr. Hunk has some significant questions to answer."

"I'd say so. He's waiting for me now. I'll report back when I get this sorted out."

"Emma, I am sorry."

She'd trusted him. "So am I. But there could be an explanation." He had promised to explain. "Let's wait and see how it turns out." If she repeated that often enough, maybe she'd heed the advice herself. It was good advice, even if at the moment, inside she was steaming-hot angry with Mason.

"One more thing before you go."

"Yeah?"

"How is the temperature holding in the HC lab?"

"Okay, so far. The ice-pack is helping. For how long? Who knows?"

"Headquarters says repairs are imminent. They're working on the auxiliary backup now. Visibility is still too bad to truck in generators."

"Do they think they can get the auxiliary up and running?"

"They do," Liz told her. "It shouldn't be long, they said."

At least that was good news. "Okay, I'll get back with you as soon as I have some answers."

"Emma, I know you feel betrayed and you're angry. I don't blame you for that. But don't you dare shoot him."

"I won't." Emma rolled her gaze.

"But you want to."

"I won't, Liz."

Emma disconnected, then took a couple deep breaths before opening the outer door. Deep breaths, and she did her best to bury the sense of betrayal that had acid pouring into her stomach. Mason better have answers for her, and he'd best not jack her around, giving them to her.

Liz knew Emma wouldn't shoot him but that she'd want to. She'd been in this position before herself, back when she worked in the field. Betrayal was never easy to take, and it could mess with your mind—*if* you let it.

Emma refused. She was in total control and intended to stay in total control. She most definitely would not shoot Mason.

But she well might make him wish she had...

CHAPTER TWENTY-TWO

Tuesday, December 18th
  1300 (1:00 PM)

Emma walked into the kitchen. Battery-lit lamps were on the breakfast bar, the counter near the sink, and on the table. Mason was pulling sliced turkey, ham and cheese out of the fridge. Mayo and mustard, pickles and chips were already on the bar. So were plates and utensils.

"There you are," he said, his tone light. "The spaghetti got commandeered by Olivia and the troops, so I'm afraid we're stuck with sandwiches."

"Works for me." Emma slid onto a bar-stool. "Honestly, I'm not fond of cold spaghetti."

"I heated it for them." He placed the cold-cuts on the bar. "Lab perk. Propane."

"Ah." She reached for the bread and began assembling a sandwich. "Is the temperature in the lab holding?"

"It's steady so far, but if we don't get power back within a couple hours, we could face some trouble." He paused to look at her. "Water, tea, or juice?"

"Tea, please."

He retrieved two bottles from the fridge and passed one to her.

"I hope it doesn't come to that," she said. "The power, I mean." That had to be the understatement of the year. "Liz says backup should be restored fairly soon." Anger that he hadn't told her about Cramer simmered in Emma. She steeled herself against it, reminding herself Mason had promised to tell her. She tossed him a lead-in to the subject. "Any word from Dr. Cramer?"

"No." Mason paused to look at her. "But honestly, he's probably gone. I doubt we'll see him again."

Well, that was a start. "In the storm? Why do you say that?"

"Olivia survived." Slathering mayonnaise onto his bread, Mason stopped, his knife in mid-air. "I don't know how Cramer would get out, but I'm guessing he had planned an exit strategy before he got here. He was only here to help in case someone got exposed—and thank God he was here."

Or Olivia would be dead. Mason was right about that. Emma loaded her bread with turkey and cheese, then slapped a second slice of bread on top of the first. "Yeah, I'm glad he was here. And that Olivia got her Christmas miracle."

"Me, too." Mason started assembling his sandwich. "He couldn't stay here. I mean, think about it. Anyone finds out, and they're all over him. He had to go."

She couldn't argue the logic in that. "I agree." Either side would snag him, especially now that he had an antidote. "You know," Emma said, swallowing a bite of sandwich and then reaching for the chips. "He looks pretty good for a corpse." She glanced over, challenging Mason. "Or would you say he's a ghost?"

"Excuse me?" Mason sat down across from her at the bar, his triple-decker sandwich on a plate in front of him.

"I mean, the man's been dead for a lot of years, so he has to be one or the other, right?" Emma snapped down on a crunchy chip.

Mason's mouth flattened into a slash. "Liz."

"Well?" Emma pushed, ignoring his supposition, though it was accurate. She took a bite of her sandwich and slowly chewed, waiting for Mason's answer.

He picked up on her upset. "You don't need to worry about him, Emma, or get defensive or hostile with me about him. Honestly. I said I'd tell you, and I intended to at first chance. The man who was here is the real Addison Cramer."

She chewed then swallowed. "You recognized him, didn't you?"

"Would I let him into the lab otherwise? Would I let him inject Olivia with an experimental drug?" Mason grunted. "Give me a little credit for having some sense."

In fairness, Mason wouldn't do either. Even angry, Emma couldn't delude herself for a second thinking he would put Olivia—any of them, really—or the lab at that kind of risk. "Explain this to me, Mason, because right now, I'm not at all comfortable with you withholding the truth from me."

"I never intended to withhold the truth from you."

"That's not an explanation," she said, her voice flat. "You did withhold—"

"Look, you're right. I delayed telling you, but I did recognize him. He was Dr. Addison Cramer."

"The dead, Dr. Addison Cramer?"

"Yes. Obviously not dead, but the same man." Mason nodded, adding weight to his claim. He paused to sip from his bottle of tea. "Think about it, Emma. Do you have any idea what would have happened to Cramer if he hadn't died that day?"

"Faked his death, you mean?"

"Yes." Frustrated, Mason dragged a hand across his nape. "Cramer had created the worst pathogen known to man—and they'd cut the antidote project." Mason lifted a hand. "He never would have agreed to develop it if they hadn't permitted the simultaneous development of the antidote. They reneged on him. If Cramer hadn't died, he would have been targeted by any number of rogue nations and special interest groups like CAR."

Mason made a valid point. "For an antidote he didn't have?"

"For the pathogen he did have in his head." Mason forced himself to drop his voice and visibly calmed down. "If he had been kidnapped by a rogue nation or a black-market group, Cramer would have been forced to replicate the virus and work on the antidote. Do you realize the jeopardy that would have put our entire nation in? The leverage the rogue nation or group with it would have against the rest of us? The entire world would have been in lethal jeopardy and held hostage."

"I can see that, yes." She could see it. Only too well. The possibility was chilling. And the odds of it happening were astronomical.

Her admission soothed the sharp edge from Mason's voice. "This field is really a pretty small community. Word gets around. When Dr. Cramer died, there were rumors."

"What kind of rumors?" She lifted her bottle and drank down some tea.

"That he'd preserved his studies," Mason said. "A lot of people searched, but no one ever found them," Mason added. "Today, he told me why."

She swallowed a bite of chip. The salt burned on her tongue. "Are you going to share that with me?"

Mason stared at her long and hard, then finally nodded. "Dr. Cramer had heard chatter that the honchos were going to cut his antidote project. He was furious and fearful. He knew what no antidote meant to him personally and to everyone else on the planet. So, he acted."

"Acted." She bit down on a crunchy pickle. "How did he act?"

"He had a makeup artist friend—they'd known each other for years—who worked on movies in LA. This guy was part of a team that developed a lot of special effects and that kind of thing."

"Does this friend have a name?"

"I'm sure he does, but Dr. Cramer didn't share it, and I didn't ask."

Probably the safest route Mason could have taken.

"Anyway," Mason went on. "This friend helped Dr. Cramer fake his suicide and disappear."

People didn't search for dead men. Only for the records he left behind. "Okay. So, the doctor disappeared and then he continued to work on the antidote. He said, privately."

"On his own, yes. In his own lab."

"Where is it?"

"I don't know."

Figured. No doubt Cramer hadn't said, and Mason hadn't asked about that, either.

He washed down a long swallow. "You know Cramer has been spotted in the airport since three days before the storm."

"I do," Emma said. "He must have a meteorologist friend, too. The storm wasn't headed here three days before the storm hit. It turned."

"But the lab is here." Mason lifted an eyebrow. "It's hard to keep locations secret in a small community." He took a bite of sandwich and slowly chewed. "Cramer kept an ear to the ground, and he suspected the lab was here." Mason held her gaze without faltering. "I have no idea who his inside source is or was, so don't bother asking. What is important is that Cramer suspected the HC lab was here and, if it was, his being here and available to help was his concern."

"I see." Cramer had taken a whale of a risk outing himself in this, especially knowing the expectation was invaders would be afoot.

"Not yet, but you're beginning to see," Mason said. "John Taylor spotted Cramer and came to me. I recognized him immediately and vouched for him."

"But you hadn't seen him close up until he showed up in the lab with me?"

"No, I hadn't. But I had spoken with him briefly on a secure phone. Before I vouched for him, I wanted to hear his voice. John Taylor handled that. I recorded Cramer and did a cross-match test via headquarters from here in the lab. Then, I vouched for him."

Obviously, the voice prints matched. "When you talked with him, what did you ask him?" Curiosity got the better of her.

"Why he was here."

"What did he say?"

"An interested party informed him of the chatter in the intelligence community and the likelihood of an attack on my lab."

"So, he did know the lab was here."

"He suspected it. The chatter proved it, my presence here affirmed it, and then Cramer's contact more or less confirmed it. Anyway, Cramer prepositioned himself here with the antidote in case it was needed."

Emma chewed that information over. Whale of a risk for him. "Are you sure it wasn't his makeup artist friend or someone else posing as Cramer?"

"I also tested his phone voice against his old lectures. Matched. I suspect his makeup artist friend had ties to the intelligence community. He died two years ago but—I'm guessing—before he died, he recruited a point-of-contact for Cramer."

Reasoned. His friend had to know Cramer needed a contact and without one, the country would be vulnerable. "Did his friend die of natural causes?" Emma hoped but doubted it.

"No. He interrupted someone tossing his home, searching for Dr. Cramer's records. The intruders tried to get the information out of him, but he didn't have it to give them. He died." Mason looked right at her. "The man here was Dr. Cramer, Em. I recognized his voice, and he was too knowledgeable to be an imposter. It was him."

"The makeup artist was... what? CIA or FBI? Assigned to one of the other alphabet agencies?"

"I have no idea." Mason admitted bluntly.

"But you're confident Dr. Cramer is gone and won't be back," Emma said. "It's your opinion that he's gone back underground."

"I expect he'll disappear and stay gone forever. It's his best chance to stay alive." Mason hiked a shoulder. "Since he left the antidote with us, his responsibility has been met. He created a danger and the means to neutralize it. His work is finally done. There's no reason for anyone to look for him now."

"Not unless the rogue nations or black-market groups discover he's alive." They had even more incentive to abduct and force him to replicate both the pathogen and the antidote now that he had a successful antidote.

"Right." Mason agreed and polished off his sandwich.

"Cramer knows that, of course."

"Now you have it. That's exactly why I expect we'll never see or hear from him again." Mason shrugged. "His only safe option is to become someone else, somewhere else. He's done all he can do, developing the antidote. His debt to society is repaid."

That was true. He hadn't violated the conditions of his agreement. He'd devoted his life since his death to continuing the work. And he'd succeeded. That was all he could do. It was definitely time for him to vanish and stay hidden. It would be hard for him. Leaving his work, which had to be the last tie he had to his old life. Imagine. Living a lifetime and one day everything familiar is gone. Her stomach hollowed and she looked at Mason. "You knew all of this before I went above and brought him back down here with me. And you let him just walk away and go."

"Wouldn't you?" Mason frowned.

She didn't answer.

Mason pushed. "Well, wouldn't you, Em?"

She thought about it. Good or bad, it wasn't a hard decision. "Yeah, I guess in this specific set of circumstances, I would have."

"You said it yourself. Too many would still want him dead or under their control. Let's be real here. Both sides want him dead. He's too big a risk to everyone alive." Mason speared another pickle then bit off a chunk. His mouth did a little pucker from the tart brine. "That was my thought."

"It's logical," she said. It chewed on her that the good guys tagged Dr. Cramer a liability as much as the bad guys tagged him as an asset. But for the nation, a planet of people, she couldn't lie and say she didn't understand their reasoning. She definitely would have let him go. To keep working after being crossed, he had to be devoted to preserving humanity. Even if located and abducted, forced to work, he'd never recreate the pathogen. He probably would recreate the antidote, praying it would render the pathogen harmless. Worthless.

Mason reached over and clasped her hand. "Do you forgive me now?"

"I understand why you did what you did and the way you did it." He hadn't refused to tell her, only delayed it. He had agreed to discuss Dr. Cramer later...

"That's not an answer to my question."

"I do forgive you." She squeezed his fingers and then loosened her grip.

He held on, lifted their hands and pressed a kiss to the back of her wrist. "Thank you for understanding."

"I do understand. That's the problem."

Mason smiled. "You definitely aren't the woman I thought you were, Em."

Exactly what he meant by that she wasn't sure. But he didn't sound disappointed. His eyes got a nice warm twinkle in them that left her breathless. "You're not who I thought you were, either." Even to her that assertion seemed absurd. She'd invested a great deal of time into studying him, thinking about him, watching him from a distance. At least, she had until the last couple of years. But her words were true.

He didn't smile but his lip curved. "Am I better or worse?"

"Better." It was true. She'd loved the young man, her girl's vision of him. She'd loved the challenge of him staying distant. He'd always intrigued her. But the man... he was so much more. So much deeper. "It does worry me that you get into all these dangerous situations and you can't shoot."

"Maybe you should teach me." He swallowed a sip of tea. "It's not that I mind being under your protection, but a couple of times during all this, you could have used some help. That I couldn't give it...that bothered me."

"You want me to teach you to shoot?" He wanted to continue to see her. After the storm. How that would work with him in Colorado and her in Atlanta, she had no idea, but for Mason, she'd make it work. "I can do that."

"Good." He smiled.

David came into the kitchen, a bounce in his step. "Olivia wants some more juice."

"How is she doing?" Emma asked.

"She's weak and tired but, from all signs, she's rebounding."

Mason smiled. "Never underestimate the power of a Christmas miracle."

"I won't ever again. I can promise you that." David poured juice into a glass then headed toward the door. "The storm is moving through. Finally." He walked out of the kitchen.

"It's good to see him not worried sick." Mason said. "That ripped my heart out."

"I don't know them nearly as well, and it got to me, too." Emma couldn't agree more. Both David and Sophia had been scared half out of their minds. Who wouldn't have been? The way they clung to each other in crisis... it was beautiful. "Are you done here?" Emma wagged a finger at their plates.

"Yes." Mason started gathering jars and stowing them back in the fridge.

Before they'd finished cleaning up the kitchen, the power came back on.

"Thank you, auxiliary team!" Emma said aloud. In the background, she could hear David and Sophia and even Jacob celebrating. He barked like Bandit.

Mason turned on the television in the adjoining sitting area. Paused to hear the latest on the weather report.

Emma joined him. "Where is Holly headed?"

"Moving toward Tinley."

"Which is where?"

"Nebraska."

"Ah." Emma turned, seeing Mason edge toward the hallway. "So where are you off to now?"

"I've got to run systems checks. Make sure the pathogens—"

"Go, go." She waved him on. "But in a minute, I want to tell you something."

He paused. "What?"

Eager, but she restrained herself. Duty first. "After the systems check."

"Is it good or bad? I've honestly about maxed out on bad, Em."

She had no idea how to answer that. He could consider her news either. "Will you go and make sure we're not all being exposed?"

"Okay." He grinned. "I'll be back."

Clearing her mind for a moment, Emma dropped down on the sofa and closed her eyes. She hadn't slept since all this started and desperately needed a power nap. At least, to rest her burning eyes until the next crisis.

CHAPTER TWENTY-THREE

1345 (1:45 PM)

THE NEXT CRISIS CAME SWIFTLY—WITHIN twenty seconds of Emma closing her eyes. It was explosive, if not an explosion. No bullets flew and no hand-to-hand combat occurred, though it ignited plenty of internal turmoil. Her mind and emotions wrestled in a battle unlike any she had ever faced. A simple thought had run through her mind, and—*boom*—it wreaked havoc and rocked her to the core.

You're still crazy about Gregory Mason Martin.

She didn't even have time to resist the thought before tumbling headlong over the edge and into an abyss. She had always been crazy about him.

No man who had treated her with indifference ever had warranted more than a notice and a footnote in her mind. None she had thought had potential and turned out not to had, either. Except for Mason. His indifference, his distance had harped on her, nagged her, bruised her heart and left it wounded in a way it never healed. All these years, she'd known the wound was there, but she'd had no idea why. Now, heaven help her, she understood why—and that her not understanding before had been a blessing.

But what did she do now? How did she handle this?

She needed to talk through it.

While she was tempted to call her mother, she didn't dare. Not with Mason still in close touch with her. Liz was the better choice.

Too agitated to sit, Emma stood and phoned Liz. As soon as she answered, Emma said, "You've got to help me."

"What's happened?"

"Don't panic. It's personal." Emma tried but failed to keep her own panic out of her voice.

"Wait one second." Liz soon came back on the line. "Okay, I've stopped the recording. Go ahead."

"I'm beyond tired. Maybe that's why I'm feeling this way."

"What way?"

"Or maybe it's the adrenaline rush from everything that's happened. Or the pressure changes from this stupid storm."

"What way are you feeling, Emma? I'm good, but you've got to give me at least a hint of what we're talking about here."

Pacing, Emma halted, stared through a spot on the wall. "I am still crazy about him."

"That's not necessarily a crisis," Liz said. "There's a reason you date and drop men, and you get engaged but never get married."

"But that's just it."

"What is it?"

"I wanted him. He never wanted me." She squeezed her eyes shut against the pain that reality shafted through her heart.

"Have you wondered why not?"

Emma's eyes shot open. "Only for most of my adult life."

"What have you figured out?"

Emma thought about it. "Honestly, I haven't figured it out. But I didn't know before that he saw the way I go through men as me thinking of men as items on a buffet."

"Did you say items on a buffet?"

"His words, not mine." Emma's face burned. She really hated admitting this, but she was all in or none on disclosure now. "I dated a lot. Nice guys mostly. But it never worked out."

"With your looks, I can see why they'd be attracted to you —and I'm getting a grip on why Mason hung back."

"Ignored. He didn't hang back. He ignored me." Emma sighed at all the nights she'd worried about what she'd done that was so wrong he couldn't stand to be around her. "He spent more time with my mother than with me. Still does apparently, the last few days aside."

"That was then. What about now?" Liz asked. Before Emma could answer, Liz went on. "He's different now, right?"

"He's said he sees me differently a couple of times."

"Are you telling me, the deep freeze has thawed?"

"Maybe. He used to think I was flighty, now he knows I'm not." Emma resumed pacing the short path between the sofa and television. "He kissed me, but that could be just a reaction to the intensity of Olivia surviving, you know?"

"That does happen. Intense emotions arise in intense situations."

"They do." Emma searched her mind, relived their inter-actions. And she kept coming back to that warm twinkle in his eyes. "Maybe that's all it is. I don't know, Liz. I'm not sure."

"That's okay."

"No. No, it is not okay."

"It is okay so long as you do something to find out," Liz countered. "So, Emma, what are you going to do to find out?"

"I don't know." Emma raised her voice. "How would I know? I don't have a clue if he's not being distant because of the circumstances here, or because he feels differently about me. It could be he's emotionally overwhelmed, too. And exhausted."

Silence.

"Liz?"

Still no answer.

Emma frowned. "Liz, are you still there?"

"I'm here. I'm trying to reconcile the woman I know you to be with the woman you're acting like right now."

"What are you talking about?"

"The woman I know takes on inserting into a foreign country to rescue an ambassador being held hostage. She handles a car exploding fifteen feet from her and never misses a step. She's smart, resourceful, competent. Pretty amazing, really. But this woman who is indecisive and confused and fears her feelings so much she denies them—that woman is a coward. She is not you, Emma."

Fury burned in Emma's stomach. "I am not a coward. Not professionally nor personally. Not in war or in peace."

Liz didn't seem at all affected by the bite in Emma's tone. "If you don't talk straight to Dr. Hunk, you are a coward."

"What?"

"Ask yourself this, Emma. All these guys with potential you've dated and been engaged to . . . What exactly did they end up lacking? Why didn't they make the cut?"

"Because they didn't. I don't know why. Relationships either work or they don't."

"You think about that. There is a reason."

"If you know it, tell me. I've been trying to figure this out forever."

"I can't tell you."

"Why not?"

"Because, Emma. Some things you need to learn firsthand. Some things you just can't tell other people. Especially about matters of the heart."

"Do you seriously think I'm a coward?"

"Not in your work, no. But personally, if you don't talk through this with him? Definitely, I do. A coward and a fool."

Emma opened her mouth to fire off a stinging retort, but the line went dead.

She couldn't believe it. Her jaw fell loose. Liz had hung up on her.

Maybe Emma should have called her mom...

But she hadn't, and she wasn't going to now. She could figure this out. As much as it galled her, Liz could be right. There had to be a reason. She wasn't a kid anymore. She was a grown woman with a good head on her shoulders. She just needed to think. As objectively as possible, she just needed to think.

Coffee. She needed coffee.

In the kitchen, she put on a fresh pot and watched it run through and fill the glass carafe. She sifted through old memories, new memories. Sifted through one relationship after another. The hope with which each of them had started. The disappointment in each of them when they had ended. Mason aside, getting a man had never been a problem. Keeping any of them had been impossible. Why?

Emma poured herself a mug of hot coffee. Smelling the steam rising off of her mug, she sat down at the bar and tried to answer that question.

Hours later, she still sat there trying to answer it, when Mason returned from the lab. The difference was all she'd reconciled in the interim. Finally, she had her answers. And though the thought of facing him with them terrified her, Emma was dead set on doing it.

"I thought you'd be sleeping." He walked over to the coffee pot. Poured himself a cup. "You okay?"

She was terrified. "I'm fine."

"Something's on your mind. Otherwise you'd be stretched out on the sofa, probably snoring."

"I don't snore," she said. "I was there. I couldn't sleep."

"Too tired?"

"Too much on my mind."

"You're okay, though, right?" His expression changed to concern.

"I'm okay. How did things go in the lab?" She wasn't avoiding the inevitable or a coward. It was just a little delay. Courage and exhaustion didn't blend well. She'd get there on it. She really would, she promised herself.

"The systems checked out okay and the temperature in the HC lab is back down to where it should be, but that doesn't mean..." He stopped then shifted subjects. "Are you getting sick, Em?"

"No, Mason."

Relief washed across his face. "Good." He slid onto the stool beside her. "There's no reason you have to stay awake. The rear wall is covered and packed, everything is okay in here, and I just talked with John Taylor. Things are all right above. Janette is in her glory, feeding all the passengers, dealing with their concerns. Well, she's getting Sam and the other vendors to feed all the passengers. The important thing is the food supply is meeting the demand."

"I know. I checked on everything about an hour ago," Emma said.

"Then what's keeping you awake?"

It was now or never. Emma glanced over at him. "You."

"What'd I do?"

"Nothing."

"Emma, you're not making a lot of sense. You really should sleep."

She frowned at him. "I want to tell you something."

"Okay." His hand curved around the mug, tightened. He clearly had no idea what was coming.

And she had no idea how he would react. "You'll probably think I'm crazy, but frankly I don't care. I'm used to you not thinking well of me."

"I've always thought well of you."

"Buffet, Mason. Did you forget that? Because I sure haven't. You know what? Never mind. It was good that you told me. It made me think."

"I didn't mean to hurt you. I was just trying to explain—"

"I don't want to go there, okay?" Emma turned on the stool to face him.

"Where do you want to go?" He didn't look upset or impatient, or as if he'd rather be anywhere else in the world instead of sitting here talking with her, their knees brushing.

"I fell in love with you in seventh grade," she said. "Did you know that?"

"No, I didn't." He wasn't just surprised. He was stunned.

"Well, I did. I knew it then, but later, when we were in college, I convinced myself I hadn't. It'd been a trick of the mind. But deep inside, in places I didn't think about because I didn't know they even existed, I knew I was in love with you. And in college, I still felt that way. Nothing ever changed that feeling, Mason." She swallowed hard. "That's why I went through men like they were items on a buffet. I kept looking and looking for the one man who would or could love me back because obviously you couldn't." The surprise on his face struck her as priceless. She managed a liquid smile. "That's what went wrong with the other men. They weren't you."

"I don't know what to say."

"You don't have to say anything." She shrugged. "I couldn't expect you to understand it. I've only just come to understand it myself. But as soon as I did, I knew it was true. That is exactly what I have been doing since seventh grade, which makes me a fool." Liz had been right. "The one man I wanted was the one man who would never give me the time of day."

To say Mason looked shocked was like saying kids are alert on Christmas morning. Gob-smacked was more accurate.

Her phone rang.

She stepped away and answered it. "Miller."

"Hey," Liz said. "Wanted you to know, authorities arrested the four. They're all identified, and all part of CAR."

"That's good news."

"They were half-buried in a snow bank about midway to Denver."

"Well, we can thank Holly for that much."

"Yeah. Power is coming back online. Tell Dr. Hunk you'll be off auxiliary within an hour."

"I will." Emma cast a sidelong glance in Mason's direction. Sober. Silent. Still. Not sure what to make of that, Emma told Liz, "The lab is secure and all systems are in the normal zone. When the roads are cleared, Mason will begin the full decontamination process."

"And what about the five thousand travelers upstairs?"

"They were never exposed," Emma said. "Airport management hasn't yet completed a full damage assessment on the facility, but they'll get the airport reopened as soon as is humanly possible."

"An advisory," Liz said. "The pathogens are being moved to a HC lab at the CDC in Atlanta."

Center for Disease Control. "Is that the right place for them?"

"Actually, it is. It's a new special access wing so that'll give added protection."

Emma's heart squeezed. "What about—"

"Don't worry about Mason," Liz said. "He's being transferred with them."

"To Atlanta?" Emma smiled. "Seriously?"

"The director thought you'd be more focused if the two of you were in the same location—when you aren't on assignment."

Now her heart thudded so hard Emma feared it'd rupture. "Are you saying my probationary period is over?" She wasn't being booted from the program!

"I am." Liz laughed. "Congratulations, Emma."

"Thank you."

"That's just a perk, I know. But I'm glad it makes you happy. Mason's the real reward."

"I couldn't agree more. We're talking now."

"How's it going?"

"I have no idea." Emma wished that weren't true. "But either way, thanks for what you said."

"You figured out the reason?"

"I did."

"Wonderful."

"I appreciate the opportunity and your help, Liz." Emma meant that sincerely.

"Not me. That came straight from the director."

"He heard that?"

"Every word," Liz said. "That was the only thing holding you back on probation. You can't run from your emotions, Em. Eventually, they'll wreck you."

Emma didn't know whether to hang her head or squeal her delight. Finally, she settled for a lame, "Thank him, also."

"You can do that yourself when you get back."

"I will." Emma hung up the phone.

Mason sat smiling. "They got them? All four in the backup team?"

"They did." Emma returned to her stool. What had changed in Mason she didn't know, but he seemed a lot more relaxed than she'd seen him in a long time.

"All is well, then?"

"I think so." She tilted her head. "Have you received word of any changes?"

"You mean about the move to Atlanta?"

He knew. She nodded.

"I was waiting until after you said what you wanted to say to tell you about it."

"You're not happy about the move?" This did not bode well.

"I wasn't sure whether it was safe to be happy. Atlanta is your town. I had no idea what you were going to say, so I didn't know if you'd welcome me there or not."

Uncertain and unsure. Like her. "It'll be easier to teach you to shoot if we're in the same state."

"True." He nodded but a smile lurked on his mouth. "So, are you done saying what you wanted to say?"

"Pretty much."

"Okay, then. My turn." He clasped her hand.

It couldn't be that bad. Not if he was holding her hand. Could it? Her heart beat fast.

"About me ignoring you," he began. "Just so you know, I went along, but that was your mother's idea."

"My mother?"

He nodded. "Her heart was in the right place. She loves you, and she liked me. She saw you going through guys and said if I was serious about you, I needed to wait until you discovered what you didn't want. Only then could you appreciate what you did." He paused, then added. "You'd come around, she said. You were smart and gorgeous, and you'd figure it out."

"Only I didn't. Not then."

"Not then, and not in college. I had hoped you would, but you didn't."

"Wait a minute. Are you saying you were interested in me way back then?"

"No, I'm saying I was crazy in love with you then, but I didn't want to be just another guy you dated and ditched. So, I kept my distance and didn't date you. I didn't want the heartbreak."

"Well, we both blew it, didn't we?"

"Did we?" He stood up and tugged her hand, suggesting she stand up. When she did, he kissed her, letting her feel his passion, his desire for her, and his vulnerability, too.

A long minute later, he parted their mouths. "Holly is over for us, Emma. We're damaged, but we made it." He stroked her cheek with a gentle thumb. "I'm thinking our personal storm is over, too."

"What exactly does that mean, Mason?"

"It means I still love you," he said simply. "I've always loved you."

Emma looked up at him and smiled. "I still love you, too."

He kissed her again. Longer, harder, and deeper.

While her senses were still reeling, he asked, "So is there an engagement you have to break before you can marry me?"

He wanted to marry her, and she definitely wanted to marry him. "Actually, no, there isn't."

"That's a relief."

"For me, too." She chuckled.

He dipped his chin. "Just so we're clear. You are saying you will marry me, right? I mean, you'll actually show up and marry me?"

She wanted to laugh. She didn't. "I will."

"I'm going to hold you to that, Emma. I mean it."

"I'm not going anywhere." She tightened her hold on his shoulders. "Everything I want is right here."

He hugged her hard.

She drew back. "In the meantime, since there's no other relationship to sever, I could help you prepare the lab."

"For what?"

"The move to Atlanta."

"Oh, honey, I have no idea when that's happening."

"According to Liz, it's happening as soon as they can get an aircraft in here to pick up the pathogens."

"Seriously?"

She nodded.

"Guess that's what the text coming in later today is going to be about. Orders for me to move to Atlanta."

"It'll be kind of convenient, since I work from there, too. It's my home base."

He smiled. "Very convenient."

"Maybe I could hitch a ride home with you and the pathogens."

His eyes were smiling. The most amazing twinkle lighting them. "Well, I don't see why not. If I heard what I think I heard, you're now a security consultant."

"Yes. Yes, I am." She curled her arms around his waist.

"So, I guess it's safe to ask the marry-or-die question now, right?"

"We'll save that for after the wedding."

"You're not going to skate out on me, are you?" Anger not uncertainty flickered across his face. "You said—"

"No way," she promised. "That's to make sure you show up and don't skate."

He laughed. "Well, no matter who your boss is, congratulations on surviving the probation, Emma."

"Thank you."

"You really are good at what you do."

"I have to be, or people get hurt. That's a strong incentive."

"It is." He dragged a fingertip along her cheek. "I loved the girl I thought you were, but I totally love the woman you've become." His voice dropped. "Who would have thought after all this time..." He didn't finish the thought. "Christmas miracles are abundant around here."

Olivia recovering. The invaders being thwarted. The lab being breached and them still keeping the pathogens contained and the contamination restricted. After three grueling years, probation was finally over and she'd been hired by Silencers, Inc. But best of all, Mason and she had finally found each other. They'd survived the deep freeze and experienced a lot of miracles in Colorado. "Definitely, abundant."

Darcy Keller appeared on the television screen beyond Mason's shoulder. Emma prayed the same would be said for Nebraska.

Mason bent to kiss her again, and a thought struck Emma. "Wait. What about David, Sophia and the kids? He'll be out of a job."

"No, he won't. They'll follow us to Atlanta. It'll take a while to sell their house and make the move. A month at most."

Emma hugged Mason hard. "I'm so glad they're coming, too."

"I'm insisting. Both David and I need to monitor Olivia long-term."

"Do you expect challenges?"

"Honestly, I don't. Dr. Cramer is doing fine, and he claims he's had no long-term effects, so we shouldn't see any in Olivia either."

"But you're taking no chances and you want to be sure."

"Exactly." Mason laughed, his smile crinkling the skin near his eyes. "We're going to build a great life together, Emma."

"If you'd said that a week ago, I would have doubted it. But after all this... I believe that we will."

And inside Emma, the remnants of the deep freeze fully thawed.

PORTAL 3 NEWS

Darcy Keller stood before the cameraman near the satellite truck in the PIA parking lot.

"Holly has left an indelible mark on Portal. Four fatalities have been reported, and two dozen injured have been transported to local hospitals. Nearly two million are currently without power.

"I've just spoken with the mayor of Portal and she reports it will take a few days before roads are cleared and people are safe to move around. For now, they're asking everyone to stay home and off the roads unless it's an emergency. Downed power lines are extremely dangerous and should be avoided. Both authorities and repair crews are braving the dangers to assess the damage. A special shout-out of gratitude to our linemen, working to get power restored, and to those from nearby areas who are coming to Portal to help. We'll share video of the damage as soon as we're able to get into those areas most heavily hit by Holly.

"Here at PIA, Assistant Airport Manager, Janette Wilson, says the facility has experienced significant damage but the five-thousand stranded passengers are all fine. One unidentified child had a raging infection, but a fellow traveler had and shared the needed antibiotics, and word is the child is out of danger and recovering. Wilson expects, barring any runway or tower damage, the airport will begin transporting passengers later this afternoon.

"We send our thoughts and prayers to the victims and their families. We also wish those injured speedy recoveries. While our nerves are frayed, there is no doubt we have much to be thankful for this Christmas. Property damages are expected to be high, but the loss of life was minimal, and while one life is a horrible price to pay, in a storm like Holly, that's a miracle.

"The storm is tracking to Nebraska. Having endured it here, my best advice is to be prepared—food, water, batteries, essential medications. You know the drill—and hunker down, Tinley and those in Holly's path. For the latest advisories and updates on Holly, stay tuned for reports from our Chief Meteorologist.

"This is Darcy Keller for Portal 3 News. Back to you in the studio..."*

Thanks for reading! If you enjoyed this book, please do leave a review.

Read on for a sneak peek of the next STORM WATCH novel, *Wind Chill* by Rita Herron.

SNEAK PEEK

WIND CHILL
STORMWATCH, Book 3
by Rita Herron

Bailey Huggins hated the cold, but she had a job to do, and today that meant braving the elements to do it. People had to be informed about the blizzard bearing down on the state and its inherent dangers or else they might get caught out in it.

The cameraman motioned for her to stand in front of the Welcome to Tinley sign so he could capture the wind battering it and the power lines as they swayed beneath the force.

She did as he instructed, then yanked her snowcap tighter over her ears, already chilled to the bone. But she was a professional trying to work her way up at the station, so as she waited to begin the segment, she pasted a smile on her face.

Rick gave her the cue, and she raised her voice so it could be heard over the roaring wind. "This is Meteorologist Bailey Huggins, reporting to you via Channel 7 news, Tinley, Nebraska. As of midnight last night, a severe weather advisory has been issued for the entire state. Holly, the worst blizzard to strike in eighty years, has already wreaked havoc on Montana and Colorado, leaving fatalities and devastation in its wake."

Thick snowflakes pummeled her, but she brushed them from her eyes with a gloved hand. "Temperatures have already dropped into the single digits and are expected to land below zero by morning, with the wind chill reaching thirty below in the next twenty-four hours." She shivered, struggling to keep her teeth from chattering.

"Road advisories have been issued, flights have been cancelled across the Midwest, and power outages are already being reported."

She paused for dramatic effect. "This is no laughing matter. People are urged to stay inside and off the roads for their own safety. Make sure you have emergency supplies available, along with food and water. Once the storm hits, roads may be impassable, businesses closed, and you won't be going anywhere."

She hesitated again, this time adding a small smile.

"Happy Holidays, folks. Unfortunately though, our White Christmas is just about to get nasty."

Chapter One
9 a.m., Gulf Shores, Alabama, December 21

Special Agent Gia Franklin was on TV again. Talking about *him*.

A smile curved his lips as he studied her smoky amber eyes, now filled with distrust and determination as she addressed the members of the press conference.

The fed was proving to be a worthy adversary. Strong-willed and smart. Calm yet menacing in the way she stared down the reporters who tossed questions at her like live grenades.

He felt like he knew her. Like she was becoming a friend. Maybe he'd forget the formalities and just call her Gia.

Just as he'd wanted to do all those years ago when she'd ignored him.

She wasn't ignoring him now.

Gia thumped her fingers on top of the podium. "I'm sorry to report that there are now nine victims of *The Christmas Killer*." A photograph of the latest female to die at his hands flashed on the screen.

Only this was a plain picture of her, not the way they'd found her. The beautiful red scarf he'd wrapped around her neck and the ornament he'd lovingly tied to her wrist were missing.

"This is Terry Ann Igley, age twenty-seven. She owned a pet grooming and boarding service that catered to tourists in this beautiful beach community of Gulf Shores," Gia continued. "If you have any information regarding her murder, please call your local police or the FBI."

His body hardened at the memory of Terry Ann's pretty dark eyes pleading with him not to kill her. She had a tender spot for all live creatures, especially dogs and cats, and was organizing a pet parade where owners dressed their furry friends in holiday costumes.

She'd trusted him.

Until she hadn't.

"When are you going to catch this guy?" a blond reporter in the front row asked.

Gia glanced at the male agent next to her, but he simply gestured for her to answer the question. It was obvious she was in charge.

"We are doing everything within our power to identify the perp and stop his killing spree. Since he has struck now in three different states, the FBI has formed a joint task force with law enforcement agencies across the states."

"He started in your home state of Florida, didn't he?" a dark-haired male reporter prodded.

The agent hesitated. Because she wasn't from Florida. Gia Franklin grew up in the small town of Tinley, Nebraska. She'd moved to Florida after her mother died three years ago, ironically right before Christmas.

She had one sibling, a sister named Carly, who still lived in Tinley, aka Tinsel Town, because each year the town hosted a huge holiday festival with activities and decorations that drew tourists from all over the region.

Carly was blonde and beautiful with the face of an angel. So opposite of her ice queen sister.

"Florida is my home now," Gia said instead. "And yes, the first three victims were from the south Florida area, then the assailant struck in Georgia."

The raven-haired reporter waved her hand. "Three kills in

Florida, three in Georgia and now three here in Alabama. He left an ornament from the Twelve Days of Christmas song with each victim. That means he's not finished."

The agent lifted her chin, anger radiating from her cool eyes. "Judging from his MO to date, I'd say that's a fair assessment. All the more reason we need anyone with information regarding the victims to come forward. No matter how small the detail, it might be helpful."

Laughter bubbled in his throat at the double meaning of the name they'd given him. *The Christmas Killer*. Fitting that he was destroying the holiday spirit for these do-gooders with his murders. All methodically planned.

His Christmases had been ruined a long time ago.

He glanced at the box of special ornaments handcrafted after the Twelve Days of Christmas song. He'd left the partridge in a pear tree ornament with his first victim. The second; two turtledoves. The third; three French hens. The fourth; four calling birds...

He still had three more ornaments to give out.

Another reporter cleared her throat. "Agent Franklin, women need to be warned. Do you have a profile of the killer?"

Gia's chest rose and fell on a deep breath, then she curled her fingers around the edge of the podium with a white-knuckled grip.

"We believe he's a white male, mid-thirties. He's methodical, organized and wants attention, as if he's staging a show by posing his victims." She swallowed. "He's charming, average to good looks, blends in with a crowd so he often goes unnoticed. In fact, that may be a sore spot with him. He feels he's invisible."

She hesitated, then cleared her throat. "While he may exhibit outward signs of violence, he possesses a dark sinister side and may be suffering from bipolar disorder coupled with manic depression. Most likely, a traumatic event occurred around this time of year in his life, so the holidays trigger his rage."

The reporter's hand shot up. "Do you have any idea where he'll strike again?"

Gia paused as if searching for answers, then stared directly into the camera. "Not at the moment. But I promise you, I won't stop until I catch him and put him behind bars."

His blood heated with admiration and...anger. Gia Franklin had just challenged him.

A chuckle rumbled from deep in his gut. She wanted to make this personal.

Hell, he'd considered making it personal before. Now he would. He'd make it *very* personal.

He snagged his phone and accessed the airlines' flight schedules. He'd planned to stay in the sunny South for the last three kills.

Now things would change, and he would up the ante. He'd skip a few states and take Gia back home. Then he'd throw her off her game.

"Nebraska, here I come," he muttered as he booked the next flight out.

Adrenaline surged through him, and he picked up another red scarf and brushed it across his cheek.

By tonight, he'd be in Tinley with Gia's sister.*

THE STORMWATCH SERIES

Holly, the worst winter storm in eighty years...

Holly blows in with subzero temperatures, ice and snow better measured in feet than in inches, and leaves devastation and destruction in its wake. But, in a storm, the weather isn't the only threat—and those are the stories told in the STORMWATCH series. Track the storm through these six chilling romantic suspense novels:

FROZEN GROUND by Debra Webb, Montana
DEEP FREEZE by Vicki Hinze, Colorado
WIND CHILL by Rita Herron, Nebraska
BLACK ICE by Regan Black, South Dakota
SNOW BRIDES by Peggy Webb, Minnesota
SNOW BLIND by Cindy Gerard, Iowa

Get the Books at Amazon

ABOUT THE AUTHOR

VICKI HINZE is the author of nearly forty novels, nonfiction books and hundreds of articles published in more than sixty-three countries. Her books have received many prestigious awards and nominations, including her selection for *Who's Who in the World* (as a writer and educator), nominations for Career Achievement and Reviewer's Choice Awards for Best Series and Suspense Storyteller of the Year, Best Romantic Suspense Storyteller of the Year and Best Romantic Intrigue Novel of the Year. She co-created an innovative, open-ended continuity series of single-title romance novels, an innovative suspense series, and has helped to establish sub-genres in military women's fiction (suspense and intrigue and action and adventure) and in military romantic-thriller novels. Hinze loves genre-blending and blazing new trails for readers and other authors. She is a former columnist for Social-In Global Network and radio host of *Everyday Woman*.

For early access to new releases and more, subscribe to the monthly newsletter at **http://mad.ly/signups/82943/join**

ALSO BY VICKI HINZE

StormWatch Series

Deep Freeze

Bringing Home Christmas

Clean Read

S.A.S.S. Unit Series

Black Market Body Double | The Sparks Broker | The Mind Thief |
Operation Stealing Christmas | S.A.S.S. Confidential

Clean Read

Breakdown Series

so many secrets | her deepest fear (Short Read)

Down and Dead, Inc. Series

Down and Dead in Dixie | Down and Dead in Even |

Down and Dead in Dallas

Clean Read

Shadow Watchers (Crossroads Crisis Center related)

The Marked Star | The Marked Bride | Wed to Death: A Shadow
Watchers Short

Clean Reads

Crossroads Crisis Center Series

Forget Me Not | Deadly Ties | Not This Time

Clean Read Inspirational

The Reunion Collection

Her Perfect Life | Mind Reader | Duplicity |
Clean Reads

Lost, Inc.

Survive the Night | Christmas Countdown |
Torn Loyalties
Clean Read Inspirational

War Games Series

Body Double | Double Vision | Double Dare | Smokescreen: Total
Recall | Kill Zone
General Audience (out of print)

The Lady Duo

Lady Liberty | Lady Justice
General Audience

Military

Shades of Gray | Acts of Honor | All Due Respect
General Audience

Paranormal Romantic Suspense

Legend of the Mist | Maybe This Time
General Audience

Seascape Novels

Beyond the Misty Shore | Upon a Mystic Tide |
Beside a Dreamswept Sea
General Audience

Other

Girl Talk: Letters Between Friends | My Imperfect Valentine |
Invitation to a Murder | Bulletproof | The Madonna Key (series co-
creator) | Before the White Rose | Invidia

Multiple-Author Collections

Dangerous Desires | My Evil Valentine | Risky Brides | Smart Women
and Dangerous Men | Christmas Heroes | Love is Murder | Cast of
Characters | A Message from Cupid Seeing Fireworks

Nonfiction Books

In Case of Emergency: What You Need to Know When I Can't Tell
You | One Way to Write a Novel | Writing in the Fast Lane | All
About Writing to Sell |

Mistakes Writers Make and How-To Avoid Them

For a complete listing visit http://vickihinze.com/books

DON'T MISS!

THE EXPLOSIVE SUSPENSE SERIES

A ground-breaking, fast paced 4-book suspense series that will keep you turning pages until the end. Reviews describe BREAKDOWN as "unique," "brilliant" and "the best series of the year." The complete series includes **the dead girl** by Debra Webb, **so many secrets** by Vicki Hinze, **all the lies** by Peggy Webb and **what she knew** by Regan Black. You'll want all four books of the thrilling BREAKDOWN series!

Printed in Great Britain
by Amazon